In memory of my grandparents,
Eunice and Arthur Talbot,
who told the best stories.

The
FAERIE
THORN

and other stories

JANE TALBOT

BLACKSTAFF PRESS

First published in 2015 by Blackstaff Press
4D Weavers Court
Linfield Road
Belfast BT12 5GH

With the assistance of
The Arts Council of Northern Ireland

© Jane Talbot, 2015
Typeset by KT Designs, St Helens, England

Printed and bound by CPI Group UK (Ltd), Croydon CR0 4YY

A CIP catalogue for this book is available from the British Library

ISBN 978 0 85640 955 4

www.blackstaffpress.com
www.janetalbotwriter.com

Follow Jane on Twitter @IntrepidJane
and on Facebook at facebook.com/JaneTalbotWriter

Contents

Introduction

At the beginning of July 2014, I took a notion to learn about tree lore.

When I read about the lore of the hawthorn, I was fascinated by its association with faeries and asked my husband if there was a lone hawthorn (known as a faerie thorn) on our farm. To my delight, he said there was, so I decided to go on a faerie-hunting expedition. I wasn't a believer, of course. I was just curious.

On the night of 5 July, I camped out near the faerie thorn. I followed standard faerie-sighting protocols, visiting the tree at evening and morning twilight, but I didn't see any faeries.

The morning visit to the tree was at around 4 a.m., so I decided to go back to sleep afterwards. When I woke up, I was astonished – and, if I'm completely honest, a little bit spooked – to find that a fully formed story about the faerie thorn was in my head!

A few days later I started writing 'The Faerie Thorn', a story which features many real places. When I finished it, I followed standard faerie-thanking protocols, returning to the thorn and leaving gifts of cream and whiskey. I wanted to offer thanks not only for the story that had magically grown in my head, but also for the more valuable gift that the story had given to me: a deeper connection to the place where I live.

I moved from Scotland to the northern part of County Antrim in 2011. Three years on, I still wasn't feeling fully at home. It was the act of writing 'The Faerie Thorn' that transformed my relationship with the place that I now call home. It brought the local landscape to life and created a bridge between me and my surroundings.

After writing 'The Faerie Thorn', I visited a range of places in the local area, many of them on the beautiful north Antrim coast, in search of inspiration for more stories.

I went to Murlough Bay and walked up to Benvan and then down to the beach and along the coast towards Fair Head, visiting the ruins of an ancient church. I visited places along the coastal stretch between Ballycastle and Portballintrae, my eye caught by an unusual white house sitting on the side of the Lannimore Hill, not far from Ballintoy. I followed the trails through Breen Wood, an ancient oak woodland just outside Ballycastle, and sat by the sea at Dunseverick harbour.

I went to Ballyness to see Saint Columb's Rill and to Bushmills to visit the distillery. By chance, when I was in Bushmills, I met the owner of the Bonner Mill, traditionally known as Curry's Mill. He showed me the water wheel and told me the story of a man who fell into it and drowned.

And wherever I went, a seed was sown and a story magically grew in my head. And the more I wrote, the greater the connection I felt to the landscape and its inhabitants, past and present.

One year on, I have a sense that I am living in a place that is full of stories waiting to be told. I feel at home – and I may actually believe in faeries too.

The
FAERIE
THORN

The First Bit

A silvery cartwheel of plump harvest moons ago, in the large mossy space between a tick and a tock, there lived a farmer called Man Donaghy. He was one of the Big People, all black-haired and broad and handsome-strong, with the dark, urgent eyes of a hungry dog.

His sparkling white cottage was nestled in a blanket of golden barleycorn all through the summer. His herd of straight-backed cattle thrived even during tough winters sent by the northern winds. The lacy ash trees made a canopy over his lush vegetable garden, letting in the perfect amount of sun and creating the perfect amount of shade.

And in a field, a potato's throw from Man Donaghy's cottage, stood a single faerie thorn.

Now, if you don't know about faerie thorns, you should. The Big People call these trees hawthorns, and in May you can see them scattering snow-blossoms in every direction. The Big People know that the Little People live in the roots of these trees, so the wisest Big People make sure that the faerie thorns are left well alone.

If a farmer has a faerie thorn on his land, he is the most lucky-unlucky man. He is lucky because the Little People play their music to the Tree Spirits, dance with the Earth Spirits and make the Air Spirits giggle. The Little People weave tumbling currents for the Water Spirits and squeeze faerie bellows for the Fire Spirits. It is the Little People who work in this way to keep all of Nature in balance. It is the Little People who make sure that the land gives her bounty to the farmer.

If a farmer has a faerie thorn on his land, he is also unlucky because it is very easy to upset the Little People. And if they get upset, they upset everything else. They can blight a crop, sour the milk of a fine dairy cow, render a horse lame and even make Big People disappear.

Man Donaghy had grown up on this farm and was well aware of the power of the tree. He always kept the field where it stood tidy, and never went close enough to get caught in an enchantment or embroiled in a faerie bargain.

▻⬩⬦⬩◦⬩⬦⬩◅

When the stars were in the right place, Man Donaghy took himself a wife. Wife Donaghy had summer in her cheeks all year round and no ache in her eyes at all. Her soft hands became worn with the hard work of a farmer's wife, but she never complained. She churned butter that sweetened everything on to which it was spread, baked bread that was lighter than air, and cooked stews that tendered even the toughest meat.

Wife Donaghy knew about the faerie thorn, but she was not afraid of it. To her, it was the most beautiful tree on the farm. Every morning twilight, when Man Donaghy went out to the fields, Wife Donaghy went down to the faerie thorn. She left a thimbleful of her husband's best poteen and a teaspoon of her smoothest cream by the roots of the thorn for the Little People, and then she sang to them as she tidied around the tree. Bundles of kindness rode the soft waves of her voice all the way down into the roots of the tree, and, after a while, the Little People came up from the Otherworld to hear her more clearly.

As she sang and moved around the tree, the Little People sprang into the curls in her red hair. They hung out of the curls like chicks from a nest, warming themselves by the good feelings in Wife Donaghy's voice.

⊱━━◦━◦━◦━━⊰

Man and Wife Donaghy ached for a child, but ten years passed with no child gifted to them. Man Donaghy became angry with his wife. He wanted sons to help him with the farm. He wanted to hand his farm over to his sons when the stars were in the right place.

Man Donaghy began to think that Wife Donaghy would never bear him a child.

He became cold and cruel to Wife Donaghy.

Man Donaghy went looking for a new wife. He went looking for a young wife.

Man Donaghy knew it would be easy to find a new wife. He had plenty of land, plenty of money, and he was double-very handsome. And soon enough, he found one in a place where no one knew him, a handful of counties away.

The woman he found in the distant county was as fresh as the dew, as sly as a fox, hungry for gold and eager to marry. All Man Donaghy needed to do now was get rid of Wife Donaghy.

><+>-0-<+>-<

As Man Donaghy rode his horse back from the distant county, the Bad Talkers in his head started whispering to him, and by the time he arrived at the farm, he had hit upon a way to get rid of Wife Donaghy.

Arriving in the darkest part of the night at the gates of his farm, Man Donaghy got off his horse and tethered it to the gatepost. He crept silently around the back of the farmhouse and over the field to the faerie thorn.

The thorn was shimmering as he knelt before it. Whispering directly to the roots of the tree, Man Donaghy said, 'I want you to take Wife Donaghy.'

Before he had even finished the sentence, Man Donaghy found himself face to face with one of the Little People. In all his forty years, he had never seen one before. The creature in front of him was big-small and mighty man-powerful. Sparks sizzled in the air around him, and, as he spoke, a hundred more Little People crowded around the roots of the tree.

'I will willingly take Wife Donaghy from you, Man Donaghy. And what will you give to me in return for my help?'

'I will give you a small sack of my gold if you take her from me.'

'Bring the gold to the tree now, and Wife Donaghy will be gone by the time that the sun has fully risen.'

Man Donaghy could hardly believe his good fortune. He rushed into the barn where his gold was hidden, brought out one small sack and left it at the roots of the faerie thorn. Then he climbed into bed with Wife Donaghy and waited.

▷─◁▷─○─◁▷─◁

Wife Donaghy was woken by a strange and beautiful sound. It was a kind of singing, but she'd never heard anything like it before. It was like the sound that stars make when they are sliding across the night sky. It was like the sound of sap rising in young trees, of flowers blossoming and of seeds beginning to sprout. It was like the sound of mauve twilight.

Wife Donaghy got up, threw a shawl over her nightgown and moved swiftly through the cottage and out into the garden, following the strains of the Otherworld song.

At the edge of the faerie thorn field she stopped to listen, and she began to recognise the song. It was the song that she had sung to the faerie thorn every morning for the last ten years.

Wife Donaghy ran to the tree, and, as soon as she was within a hare's ear of its roots, she disappeared.

The Next Bit

Man Donaghy brought New Wife Donaghy to the farm. She was a fine-looking woman with thick, straight, chestnut hair and linen-white skin. She suited her apron well, but she did not suit the work of a farmer's wife. She spent Man Donaghy's money as quickly as she could and did as she pleased when her husband was out in the fields.

New Wife Donaghy did not tend the faerie thorn, and Man Donaghy let the field in which it stood grow wild with dock leaves. He did not want to go anywhere near the tree for fear that his old wife would reappear or that the Little People would ask for more gold.

Every harvest moon for three years the belly of New Wife Donaghy grew big, but no new Big People arrived into the world – not breathing ones anyway. Man and New Wife

Donaghy buried their almost-but-not-quite sons beneath the ash canopy. They prayed for the Memory Takers to help them to forget the pain, but you and I both know that the Memory Takers cannot take such memories away.

On the night of the harvest moon, exactly one year after they had buried their third almost-but-not-quite son, new Wife Donaghy was sitting under the ash canopy when she saw an old woman creeping in the shadows.

'What are you doing on Donaghy's ground, old woman?' spat New Wife Donaghy. 'What is your business here so late in the evening?'

New Wife Donaghy did not warm-welcome this stranger. She offered her neither food nor drink. The old woman was cloaked, hooded and bent over, and she had the look of a knows-everything woman.

Now, if you don't know what a knows-everything woman is, you should. A knows-everything woman is not really one of the Big People. She is one of the Little People who knows how to make herself look like she is one of the Big People, and she weaves spells with her bare hands. If a knows-everything woman touches you, or if you touch her, you'll be in mighty big trouble. You really have to have proper seeing eyes to recognise a knows-everything woman before it's too late.

I don't think New Wife Donaghy had her seeing eyes open in the autumn moonlight under the ash trees that evening.

'I'm just a weary old woman looking for a place to sit down for a while. If you could just help me to the bench by your window, I'll take a breath or two, and then I'll be on my way.'

Reluctantly, New Wife Donaghy offered her arm to the crooked crone and helped her over to the bench. As the old woman sat down, she looked up into New Wife Donaghy's eyes in a knows-everything way.

'My, those eyes have seen a lot ... maybe even too much,' remarked the old woman. And, as she said those words, she raised her frail hand to touch New Wife Donaghy's face.

'And your teeth ... my, they'd be enough to sharpen any tongue.' And, as she said those words, the old woman moved her hand to New Wife Donaghy's mouth.

'And your hair ... my, that's thick enough to cover all sorts of mischief.' And, as she said those words, the old woman moved her hand to New Wife Donaghy's hair.

'And your belly ... my, three almost-but-not-quites. That must be painful.' And, as she said those words, the old woman moved her hand down to New Wife Donaghy's belly.

'You seem to know a lot about me, old woman,' said New Wife Donaghy, all sharp and suspicious.

'Oh, New Wife Donaghy, I know everything.' And with that, the old woman creaked herself up off the bench and shuffled off into the shadows. New Wife Donaghy noticed the slugs and snails hanging from the hem of the old woman's cloak, the whiff of sour milk in the air and the glistening trail she left behind her.

Now New Wife Donaghy's seeing eyes were open, but it was too late.

The Horrible Bit

As the tickling, mauve twilight roused Man Donaghy the following morning, he turned to greet New Wife Donaghy and jumped clean out of his skin.

'Foul creature, what have you done with New Wife Donaghy?' roared Man Donaghy, half-angry, half-afraid.

The creature was shocked awake by Man Donaghy's cries and sat bolt upright in bed.

'Oh, Man Donaghy, I cannot see you properly. Why is there a fog hanging in our room? Chase it away, you fool, so that I may see!' As the creature spoke, a hot serpent tongue whipped in and out of its mouth, slicing the skin on its face and scorching the linen of the bed.

'Is that you, New Wife Donaghy?' tremble-whispered Man Donaghy.

'Of course it's me, you idiot!' hissed the white-eyed creature.

'If it is you, New Wife Donaghy, why is your hair so wiry-wild and grey? It looks like a thunderstorm passed straight over your head last night and sent a bolt of lightning to your locks.'

New Wife Donaghy put her hands to her head, and, as she did, scuttleroaches tumbled from each dirty curl.

'If it is you, New Wife Donaghy, why is your belly as big as a gorse-ale barrel?'

New Wife Donaghy put her hands to her belly, and, as she did, she was gripped by a fiery, contracting pain. It felt like three new Big People were trying to cut themselves out of her belly all at once.

New Wife Donaghy screamed a Hell scream.

>-+-+>-0-<+-+-<

Three more harvest moons came and went. Every day, New Wife Donaghy gulped from the poteen pot from dawn until dusk to soothe her pain. Raw, bald patches appeared on her head where the scuttleroaches hatched out of her skull. Her eyes fell out, leaving gaping holes where the roaches scratched for food. Her serpent tongue grew sharper by the day, and her belly never gave her any peace.

Every day, Man Donaghy was lashed by his wife's serpent tongue. Every day, he sweat-toiled in the fields from dawn until dusk, but in spite of his hard work, the farm started to fail. In the vegetable garden, the runner beans stopped running. The barleycorn was blighted within a day of pushing through the soil. The cattle died. The earth grew sour and the well water became bitter.

The only field that remained growing-green was the field in which the faerie thorn stood.

One day, seven harvest moons after the Little People had taken Wife Donaghy, New Wife Donaghy lashed Man Donaghy so harshly with her serpent tongue that the Bad Talkers began to whisper in his head again, just as they had on his way back from the distant county. *Man Donaghy, New Wife Donaghy has blighted your land*, they said. *New Wife Donaghy is word-beating you so hard that, if she continues, you will not see the year out. Go to the Little People and ask them to take her away too.*

Man Donaghy heeded the words of the Bad Talkers, and, on the first night of November, he made sure that New Wife Donaghy took even more greedy gulps of his best poteen than usual. When she was grizzle-snoring, he slipped out of bed and out of the cottage, across the field to the faerie thorn.

The thorn was shimmering as he knelt before it. Whispering directly to the roots of the tree, Man Donaghy said, 'I want you to take New Wife Donaghy.'

Before he had even finished his sentence, Man Donaghy found himself face to face with one of the Little People. He was big-small and mighty man-powerful and sparks sizzled in the air around him. Man Donaghy recognised the creature: he was the one he had bargained with before, but this time he wore a dock-leaf crown.

'I would willingly take New Wife Donaghy from you, Man Donaghy, but I am afraid that there is no longer any space in my Otherworld kingdom beneath this tree.' As he spoke, a hundred Little People appeared around the roots of the tree, along with the bent-over old woman with the cloak hemmed with slugs and snails.

'Wife Donaghy has filled our kingdom with kindness; she sings honey into every nook and cranny, and plants good feelings that grow from the bottom of our kingdom to the edge of your world. There is no space here.' As the dock-crowned creature spoke these words, a vision of Wife Donaghy appeared beside him. She too wore a dock-leaf crown over her lively, red curls. Her belly was child-swollen, and the Time Winders had tick-tocked the Big Clock very slowly for her: she looked as if she had not aged a day since she had been taken.

'Oh, what am I to do?' wailed Man Donaghy.

'Well, I can make arrangements for the trolls at the Gortanuey Bridge to take her instead, but, in return, you must give me your farm. Bring the deeds to your land to me tonight, then take New Wife Donaghy to the bridge, and the trolls will take her from you.'

Man Donaghy was so relieved at the prospect of being

freed from New Wife Donaghy that he agreed immediately. He ran into the cottage to get the deeds and brought them back to the faerie thorn within minutes.

New Wife Donaghy was still grizzle-snoring as he loaded her into his cart. He drove hard and fast into the night until he reached the Gortanuey Bridge.

The Tricky Bit

Now, if you don't know about trolls, you should. Trolls live under bridges and guard them well, and if you happen to pass under a bridge where trolls are living, they'll guard you well too. They'll take you to the other side of the Seeing Curtain where you can see out, but no Big People can see in. They will weave troll magick all around you like a binding weed, but you won't realise that you are being bound. They will keep you stumbling-drunk on elderberry wine and sleepy-full on rabbit stew. They will make your thoughts curl with their music and stories. And then, when you are bound so tight that your nose can barely wrinkle itself, they will tell you to look out through the Seeing Curtain and show you how many full moons have passed. They will show you what has been taken from you, and then they will tear the beating heart from your body and make you dead-alive so that you have to stay in the In-Between Place – for ever.

So if you go to a bridge where trolls live, do not accept their hospitality – the invitation is a trick to make you pass through the Seeing Curtain. And if you pass through the Seeing Curtain, you will never return. If you go to a bridge where trolls live, you must have your seeing eyes open at all times.

⊱─━━◦─◦━━─⊰

Man Donaghy was so keen to get rid of New Wife Donaghy that he did not have his seeing eyes open that night. As soon as he got to the Gortanuey Bridge, he jumped off his cart and dragged New Wife Donaghy all the way down the slurry-sodden verge, until he was right underneath the bridge.

He stood in the stream that ran beneath the bridge and whisper-shouted, 'Trolls, I have come with New Wife Donaghy!'

Before Man Donaghy had finished his sentence, a small, squat figure waddle-stomped out from the shadows beneath the dank, dripping archway of the bridge. He was holding up a torch and looking very disgruntled. The folds of his face were trench-deep, he had ten-to-four eyes, and his beard was all peated-up. A leg of something that was still moving hung out of the corner of his mouth.

'Who comes a-gowling at our bridge at this time of night?' spat the troll. 'You are interrupting our supper!'

'It is Man Donaghy. I believe arrangements have been made, have they not?' Man Donaghy's voice was shaky-scared. The troll was so ugly that the bottom half of Man Donaghy wanted to run away, but the top half of Man Donaghy was so desperate to get rid of New Wife Donaghy that it made the bottom half stay put.

'Hmmm … They may well have been made, but this is a mighty inconvenient time. If you want us to take New Wife Donaghy right now, you'll have to bring her inside yourself as we are still a-troughing, and we want to eat our supper while it's still alive.'

Man Donaghy did not stop to think. He hauled slurry-mudded New Wife Donaghy into the trolls' cave behind the Seeing Curtain.

'Just leave her on that rug by the fire, she'll soon dry out. And you, Man Donaghy – from what we hear, you must be soul-worn tired. Sit down and take a sup of our fine elderberry wine. There's rabbit stew in the pot by the fire, too – take as much as your belly needs,' said the troll with the ten-to-four eyes and the peated-up beard.

Man Donaghy found the invitation mighty hard to resist. New Wife Donaghy had not looked after his belly for years – she had been too busy tending her own.

He looked over to the table and saw two more trolls. One

had a hairy-warted pig snout and a long, ratty tail. The other was all grubbymuckit and had rusty-nail teeth. Both trolls had snotterworms hanging from their noses. They were busy slack-jaw-eating their wriggling supper and entertaining themselves by doing farts that were too big to sit on.

Man Donaghy ladled himself a bowl of stew, took a chair at their table and started to eat. It was the most delicious stew he had ever tasted. He took a ram's horn of wine. It was the sweetest, most berrysome wine he had ever drunk.

Every time he emptied his bowl, the trolls magicked it full again. Every time he drained the ram's horn dry, the trolls magicked it full again.

The three trolls beady-eyed-up Man Donaghy. The grubbymuckit troll with the rusty-nail teeth was the first to speak.

'We've had a few of you Big People sit at our table with us, Man Donaghy, but most of them are just passing through.' The troll nodded in the direction of a set of enormous, en-graved oak doors at the back of the cave. 'They are usually heading for the other side of those doors.'

'What is on the other side of them?' asked Man Donaghy as he downed another ram's horn of elderberry wine.

'A Hell Gate. And that Hell Gate is mighty feary and even uglier than we are, so we hid it behind something pretty. That way, when Big People arrive here, and they're heading in that direction, it doesn't look so feary. We are good at guarding things, so we guard the Hell Gate. In return, our fire is kept burning.'

Man Donaghy must have started to smell frightened because the troll with the pig snout and ratty tail chipped in. 'Relax, Man Donaghy. You are not heading in that direction. Not yet, anyway. Nor is New Wife Donaghy. Not yet, anyway.'

Man Donaghy breathed a sigh of relief and raised the ram's horn to his berry-stained lips once more. And as the fire dried out New Wife Donaghy, her sharp serpent tongue was the first part of her to awaken.

'Man Donaghy, what have you done with my fine dress, you fool? I smell all slurried-up. And where are we? This doesn't sound like the cottage. I didn't tell you to move me anywhere. How dare you move me in my sleep!'

Man Donaghy began to laugh from his belly. 'Oh, New Wife Donaghy, I am so tired of your word-beating, and of waking up with scuttleroaches on my pillow that I am leaving you with the trolls. I will never have to feel the sharpness of your tongue again.'

Then all three trolls started to laugh from their bellies and shook their heads in delight.

'Oh, Man Donaghy, do you not realise that you are behind the Seeing Curtain and that you cannot leave?' The troll with the pig snout and the ratty tail guffawed. 'Do you not realise that you have already been here for seven full moons?'

'I have not been here for one full night,' insisted Man

Donaghy, 'and New Wife Donaghy could not possibly have slept for seven full moons.'

The trolls snort-giggled, and the grubbymuckit troll with the rusty-nail teeth held up a small pouch. 'Sleep clover, Man Donaghy. She's lying on a rug made of sleep clover!'

'It's true,' said the troll with the ten-to-four eyes and peated-up beard. 'Let us take you to the Seeing Curtain, and you can see for yourself.'

The Things-Couldn't-Get-
Any-Worse Bit

Man Donaghy stood nose-close to the Seeing Curtain as the troll with the ten-to-four-eyes and peated-up beard showed him the farm that he had traded for the taking of New Wife Donaghy.

Man Donaghy saw how the fields swayed golden, bursting with fat barleycorn. Man Donaghy saw a new herd of handsome cattle grazing on sweet, thick, emerald grass. Man Donaghy saw runner beans sprinting up garden canes.

'It's a fine farm, Man Donaghy,' said the troll. 'Do you want to see more?'

'Show me everything, troll,' said Man Donaghy.

Man Donaghy saw the faerie thorn field, all tidied like a Sunday-best suit. Man Donaghy saw the sparkling white cottage, draped in swathes of briar roses the colours of summer sunsets.

And then, under the ash tree where the three almost-but-not-quites were buried, Man Donaghy saw Wife Donaghy. She sat peacefully with her red curls tumbling on to her shoulders, a nursing baby in her arms and the shade of the tree moving for her like a willing servant.

'Wife Donaghy has my farm?' asked Man Donaghy.

As soon as the words 'Wife Donaghy' had been spoken, the two trolls who were still at the table spat out their food and walloped their way to the Seeing Curtain.

'Where is she? Where is she? Where is she?' asked the troll with the pig snout and the ratty tail.

'She's there, under the ash tree,' swooned the troll with the ten-to-four eyes and the peated-up beard.

'Sing! Sing! Sing, Wife Donaghy!' begged the grubbymuckit troll with rusty-nail teeth.

Wife Donaghy did not sing. Instead, it seemed as if she turned to look directly at Man Donaghy through the Seeing Curtain. And as she turned, glints of starry light shimmered around her.

'What is that light?' puzzled Man Donaghy.

'Oh, you know him! That is the dock-crowned King of The Faerie Thorn. He is the father of Wife Donaghy's boy child.

That child will become one of those mighty Big-Little People,' answered the grubbymuckit troll with the rusty-nail teeth.

Man Donaghy's heart sank so low that it was almost peeking out from beneath his ribs.

'And why do you all want Wife Donaghy to sing?' asked Man Donaghy.

'Have you not heard Wife Donaghy sing, Man Donaghy?' asked the troll with the ten-to-four eyes and the peated-up beard.

Man Donaghy shook his bewildered head.

The troll with the ten-to-four eyes and peated-up beard then opened his tattered leather jerkin and took out a tiny box, the size of a thumbnail, from one of his inside pockets. He opened the box and took out a single ear of golden barleycorn. He signalled to Man Donaghy to bend down and then held up the ear of barleycorn to Man Donaghy's ear. All three trolls pushed their own hairy ears up towards Man Donaghy's so that they could listen too.

The three trolls and Man Donaghy stood all magicked-up as they listened to the singing from the ear of barleycorn. The voice was as sweet as gorse flowers. It sang warm summer breezes and reached the place where everyone begins and where everyone ends.

At the end of the song, all three trolls fell into a big heap of swoon, drunk on good feelings.

At the end of the song, Man Donaghy's heart was so

heavy that it fell right into the softest part of him.

><+<>-O-<>+<

Man Donaghy wanted to look through the Seeing Curtain once more but the picture had disappeared. He heard the serpent tongue of New Wife Donaghy cutting and lashing from the fireside. He smelled the slurry stench of her dress. He turned to see her brushing scuttleroaches on to the hearth from her head.

And as Man Donaghy horrored at his predicament, the troll with the ten-to-four eyes and peated-up beard spoke gently to him. 'Man Donaghy, your heart is woeful heavy.'

As he heard the troll's words, Man Donaghy looked down and saw that the troll had his hand right inside his body. He was holding Man Donaghy's heart.

The troll ripped Man Donaghy's beating heart out of his body and said, 'Now you are dead-alive and you must stay here with us in the In-Between Place.'

Man Donaghy's eyes filled with sadness. 'How long must I stay in the In-Between Place?'

'You must stay here until the moons stop sailing across the night skies and the sun never rises again,' stated the troll, all matter-of-fact.

Suddenly, the look in Man Donaghy's eyes turned from sadness to horror.

'You mean, I am trapped with New Wife Donaghy in the In-Between Place for ever?' wailed Man Donaghy.

And then it happened. The Know-It Hammer struck the head of each of the trolls hard. They, too, would be stuck for ever with New Wife Donaghy and her lashing serpent tongue.

The eyes of the troll with the peated-up beard panic-whizzed from ten-to-four to ten-past-eight and back again.

Sleep clover was hard to come by and very expensive, so they could not make her sleep until the sun stopped rising.

Earfuls of Wife Donaghy's voice would give them relief for the length of a song, but these were also expensive, and the trolls' earful account with the Faerie Thorn King was already well overdrawn. Indeed, they had taken New Wife Donaghy, at the request of the King, in an attempt to reduce their debt. The trolls had but three earfuls left, and that would not be enough song to save even one of them from the awful earful that New Wife Donaghy would give them.

Now the trolls were in as much trouble as Man Donaghy, and they knew it. The troll with the ten-to-four eyes and peated-up beard ordered the other two trolls to follow him that very instant.

In great haste, all three trolls waddle-stomped through the Seeing Curtain.

'Open your hairy ears, brothers,' said the troll with the ten-to-four eyes and the peated-up beard. 'We need a good troll trick, because if we don't do something we will either have to live in the In-Between Place with New Wife Donaghy for ever, or leave our bridge and our fire. I like our bridge and our fire, and Hell Gates are mighty hard to come by in these parts. All the good ones are already taken.' The alarm in his voice worried the other two trolls and they huddled together in urgent troll trick talks.

Now, if you don't know about troll tricks, you should. A troll trick is a bargain which looks not only fair but also big-pocket generous. But be warned – when a troll trick is played, the troll always wins, and the bargain is neither fair nor generous. You must never bargain with a troll because if you do, you will lose. Usually, you will lose everything.

If you meet a troll or three, you must always keep your hearing ears open so you can hear the troll trick coming. Man Donaghy felt so wretched that he did not have his hearing ears open that night.

━━━━◦━◦━◦━◃

The Gortanuey Bridge trolls cunninged-up a bargain that would not only help them to keep their bridge and get rid of New Wife Donaghy, but would also give them something that they could trade. The bargain would give them something that they could use to pay off their debt to the Faerie Thorn King and get at least a field of Wife Donaghy's earfuls.

The three trolls pushed their way back through the Seeing Curtain and waddle-marched up to Man Donaghy, standing right under his nose. They put on their best we-like-you faces and started their troll trickery.

'Man Donaghy, you are right. You have already suffered a full blow of woe, and we would like to stop New Wife Donaghy from word-beating you – for ever. We will make the arrangements for the Hell Gate to open and for the Below King to take her, but it will cost you,' said the grubbymuckit troll with the rusty-nail teeth.

Man Donaghy started to sob. 'Oh trolls, how kind you are to offer me such a thing, but I am afraid that I have nothing left to give. I have lost everything.'

The troll with the pig snout and ratty tail shook his head and smiled a pretend you-can-trust-me smile. 'Man Donaghy, you have not lost everything. There is something that we would be happy to take from you in exchange for New Wife Donaghy's passage through the Hell Gate.'

'What is it that I could give you?' puzzled Man Donaghy.

All three trolls smiled real smiles and rubbed their hands together.

The Things-Actually-Get-A-Lot-Worse Bit (which includes The Really Gruesome Bit)

'You still have your good Big People looks and your fits-like-a-glove skin, Man Donaghy. In exchange for New Wife Donaghy's passage through the Hell Gate, we will take your black hair, your broad, strong bigness and the bloodline gift that brings handsomeness to the face of all your kin. We will also take your manly farmer skin that you have kept young by sweat-toiling in the fields,' answered the troll with the pig snout and the ratty tail.

Man Donaghy was deep-ditch desperate. Sunk in a heap on the floor, he was already nodding his head before the troll had finished explaining the full consequences of the agreement. He was already nodding his hurting head before his thinking head had worked out what, if anything, he would be left with.

'No time like the present, Man Donaghy! We'll take your good Big People looks and your fits-like-a-glove skin right now and start making the arrangements with the Below King.' As the grubbymuckit troll with the rusty-nail teeth said these words, he reached out and pulled at Man Donaghy's thick, black hair.

A scorching pain seared its way beneath Man Donaghy's

skin and scraped across every inch of his bones. The grubbymuckit troll with the rusty-nail teeth stood in front of Man Donaghy and held up the full bloody skin of him in his dirty hands to inspect it.

The troll with the ten-to-four eyes and peated-up beard nodded approvingly at the skin and then turned to address Man Donaghy. 'Now you are right, Man Donaghy. *Now* you have lost everything. You have lost beautiful Wife Donaghy, who would have brought great wealth to you with her voice and great luck to you as she is loved by the Little People. You have lost the chance of an heir, and you have lost your farm. And now you have lost your good Big People looks and your fits-like-a-glove skin. Now you are nothing but a bone-ghost.'

Now, if you don't know what a bone-ghost is, you should. Bone-ghosts are dead-alive, but only a little bit alive and a lot dead. They are Big People whose hollow souls are trapped for ever in the In-Between Place. Their charred skeletons are covered here and there with rotting, smoking flesh, they have no hair and they are frightening-ugly – the kind of ugly that would make your heart stop beating. Just. Like. That.

If you are one of the Big People, and you see a bone-ghost, it is already too late. Your heart will stop beating. Just. Like. That.

To be really safe, you'll need to have your smelling nose

wide open – the rotting stench of a bone-ghost hangs around it like a putrid cloud. If you smell a bone-ghost, run!

⊁⊶⊷⊙⊶⊷⊰

'What is that awful smell? Trolls, clean your house at once!' scolded New Wife Donaghy.

'We would clean it if we had time, New Wife Donaghy, but we don't. You see, we've been thinking – it must have been stone hard having to put up with such a useless husband for all these years, so we think you deserve a little trip. It's the least we can do,' schmoozled the troll with the ten-to-four eyes and the peated-up beard. 'We've an … *acquaintance* who'd appreciate your good company.'

'Trolls, you are right. It's been hell.' New Wife Donaghy's sharp serpent tongue blunted a little as it licked up the clever-kind words of the troll.

'New Wife Donaghy, it has definitely not been Hell, but it has been hard for you. Our … *acquaintance* isn't such a good cook, though – he tends to burn things – so you had best take a bowl of rabbit stew and a glug of elderberry wine before we go. And be quick about it. We really need to get going.'

New Wife Donaghy did exactly as she was told. She was so keen to go on her trip, and to get away from the terrible smell of her bone-ghost husband, that she hurried herself along.

She lifted a bowl of rabbit stew to her face and lashed the contents into her mouth with her serpent tongue, spattering tasty juice up over her cheeks and down on to her spiky-haired chin. The scuttleroaches rode the helter-skelter ride of her wiry curls all the way down her face to clean up the leftovers.

New Wife Donaghy guzzled down a ram's horn of wine and burped like a troll.

'Right, I'm ready trolls,' declared New Wife Donaghy.

'Perfect! Now, as you cannot see, and as your sore belly is so heavy, let my two brothers support you,' schmoozled the troll with the ten-to-four eyes and the peated-up beard.

'At least someone knows how to treat a lady properly, Man Donaghy!' hissed New Wife Donaghy, not knowing quite in which direction to send her word-beating.

As the troll with the pig snout and ratty tail and the grubbymuckit troll with the rusty-nail teeth shuffled New Wife Donaghy towards the enormous, engraved oak doors, the troll with the ten-to-four eyes and peated-up beard beckoned Man Donaghy. He signalled for Man Donaghy to open one door while he opened the other.

The heavy doors creaked open and the Hell Gate stood before them.

It was a thousand times more frightening than a bone-ghost. The screams that came from the other side of the gate were so soul-empty that they could drive a madness worm straight into your skull, and the heat was enough to melt cauldron iron.

The troll with the ten-to-four eyes and peated-up beard nodded to his brothers and, as they pushed New Wife Donaghy towards the Hell Gate, he said, 'Now this, New Wife Donaghy, is definitely Hell.'

New Wife Donaghy's skin snagged on the razor-edged railings of the Hell Gate. Smoking fire claws gripped at her ankles. Her slurried-up dress blazed and burned into her body. Her skin started to melt like candle wax, and flames roared through her eye sockets. The scuttleroaches sizzled and crisped in her fireball hair.

New Wife Donaghy screamed a Hell scream.

'Enjoy your trip!' shouted Man Donaghy. The trolls fell into a giggle heap, and Man Donaghy even managed a smile.

But not one of them had thought to close the enormous, engraved oak doors behind them. And just as Man Donaghy started to see the shiny edge of some kind of freedom, New Wife Donaghy's hot serpent tongue slither-whipped out through the doors, grabbed him around his bone-ghost throat like a shepherd's crook and pulled him through the Hell Gate.

The Last Bit

The trolls wasted not a single tick-tock of time. They scrubbed up Man Donaghy's good Big People looks. They ironed his fits-like-a-glove skin. And as soon as the looks and the skin were ready, they took them to the Faerie Thorn King.

▸—◆—○—◆—◂

'Faerie Thorn King, it must be heart-sore painful for you to be with your beautiful wife and yet not be able to feel her skin or hold her soft Big People body. It must be heart-sore painful for you not to be able to feel the weight of your own child in your arms,' said the troll with the ten-to-four eyes and peated-up beard in his most respectful voice.

'You are right, troll. Until I have a borrow-body, I must endure this pain,' sighed the Faerie Thorn King.

The trolls tried their best to contain their greedy excitement and stop themselves from waddle-hopping on the spot. But they couldn't.

Now, the Faerie Thorn King was one of the cleverest Little People in the whole of the Otherworld. He was so clever that he had thoughts that were much bigger than his own head. He knew that the trolls wanted something. He was suspicious of a troll trick being played and had his hearing ears wide open.

'I hear a troll trick coming. If you trick me, trolls, I will make arrangements for you all to stay with the Below King – for ever. New Wife Donaghy is giving him such a lashing with her serpent tongue that he's been buying Wife Donaghy's earfuls from me at a devilish rate. His earful account is well overdrawn – just like yours. He owes me many favours.'

'Oh my Lord, King of the Faerie Thorn! We know your mighty power stretches below, between and above. We will not trick you. We have come to pay our debt with something that you will like,' said the troll with the ratty tail, bowing down to press his hairy-warted pig snout on the floor and thrusting his filthy buttocks high in the air.

'Your debt is as large as the sky, trolls. How will you pay me?' asked the Faerie Thorn King.

'We have what you need, my Lord. We have a borrow-body for you with very good Big People looks,' said the grubbymuckit troll with the rusty-nail teeth, holding up the good looks and fits-like-a-glove skin of Man Donaghy.

'See, we got the whole borrow-body *and* the good Big People looks!' The troll with the pig snout and the ratty tail could not contain his pride for one moment longer.

The Faerie Thorn King began to shimmer brightly as he saw the borrow-body with the good Big People looks. The trolls could see the want-it in his eyes.

'If you clear our debt, we will give you the borrow-body,'

wilied the troll with the ten-to-four eyes and the peated-up beard.

The want-it was so big in the Faerie Thorn King that he agreed to the bargain immediately.

The troll with the ten-to-four-eyes and the peated-up beard now stood a little taller. 'Good,' he continued smugly. 'That is fair. Obviously, the good Big People looks are a separate item. Would you like to buy them from us too?'

The Faerie Thorn King laughed at their cheek, but was not angry. He admired the trolls' cunning and sore-wanted the good Big People looks.

'What do you want for the looks?' enquired the Faerie Thorn King.

'We want two things, my Lord. Number one thing: do not send us to the Below King. Number two thing: give us a whole harvest field of Wife Donaghy's earfuls.'

The Faerie Thorn King nodded and the deal was done.

><>-O-<><

From that day forward, Wife Donaghy and the Faerie Thorn King lived together with their son in the sparkling white cottage on their thriving farm. Wife Donaghy taught their son the ways of the Big People and the Faerie Thorn

King taught him the ways of the Little People. And so their son, Boy Donaghy, grew into one of those mighty Big-Little People that the trolls had talked of. He was mighty man-powerful and sparks sizzled in the air around him.

Boy Donaghy knew how to sing to the Tree Spirits, dance with the Earth Spirits and make the Air Spirits giggle. He knew how to weave tumbling currents for the Water Spirits and squeeze faerie bellows for the Fire Spirits. He knew how to help things to grow and how to gentle-birth the fruits of the land. Boy Donaghy knew how to talk with the Big People and with the Little People. He knew how to be kind, he knew how to be clever, and he knew how to work farmer-hard.

And when the stars were in the right place, Boy Donaghy became New Man Donaghy and took over the farm. The farm prospered and so did he.

And when the stars were in the right place, the Big People heart of Wife Donaghy stopped beating. The Faerie Thorn King buried her Big People body next to the faerie thorn tree and grew an elder above it so that the roots would surround and protect her, and so no one could borrow-body her or steal her good Big People looks.

The Faerie Thorn King took off his borrow-body and buried it beneath the ash tree next to the three almost-but-not-quites.

Then the Faerie Thorn King took Wife Donaghy's soul into the roots of the faerie thorn tree and sang to it until it woke up. He sang to it until Wife Donaghy sang back. And as they sang together, the elder and faerie thorn intertwined so that the Faerie Thorn King and Wife Donaghy could hold each other above the ground and below the ground – for ever.

The Extra Bit

Even the Time Winders have lost count of the number of harvest moons that have passed since Wife Donaghy's heart stopped beating. And any Time Winder will tell you that the sky has changed whole constellations since then and that it's not so easy to find the large mossy space between the tick and the tock any more.

Some of the old-ways-wise Big People say that the only way you'll find the space between the tick and the tock is to have your proper seeing eyes and hearing ears open at the mauve time of day.

If you ever find that space at the mauve time of day, stand in front of the intertwined faerie thorn and elder tree behind Donaghy's cottage, and you will see the Faerie Thorn King and Wife Donaghy dancing.

If you ever find that space at the mauve time of day, stand underneath the ash tree that shades Donaghy's vegetable garden, and you will feel the three almost-but-not-quites turning over in their sleep, right under your feet.

If you ever find that space at the mauve time of day, stand in one of the golden barleycorn fields at Donaghy's farm when the twilight breeze is curling through the ears of the crop, and you will hear Wife Donaghy singing.

If you ever find that space at the mauve time of day, stand on the Gortanuey Bridge, and you will hear the hot serpent tongue of New Wife Donaghy word-beating the Below King and Man Donaghy.

And if you dare to climb under the arch of the bridge, and if you bump into a troll or three, remember to keep your seeing eyes and hearing ears WIDE open, won't you?

The STORY
of AMERGIN

The Birth of Amergin

In the before-time, when all stories were true and magick worked powerful strong, there lived a talented smith called Eccet. His work was so revered that every man in Ulster wanted an axe or a sword that had been forged by his clever hands.

Eccet could work metal like no other smith. He could put his big, bare hands into a forge fire without getting burned, and he used his firm fists to hammer out the metal. He used his fine fingernails to engrave artful embellishments, the form of which no eye had seen before. He whispered wit to the metal to make it shine, and the weapons he wrought brought battle fortune to every army that wielded them.

Eccet's dwelling and forge sat side-by-side on the banks of the River Bush, and he lived in that place with his wife, Gelace, and his daughter, Asna.

Gelace was fine-limbed and swan-necked and glowed with good-heart kindness. So awake was her soul that her feelings livelied in her and all about her and coloured her face like the roof of Heaven.

Asna was nine winters old and knew how to speak with the birds. She could sing the sound of dawn, the call of wintering and the promise of summer, and every night when she slept she hooted the lonely song of the long-eared owl.

Eccet and Gelace heart-ached for more children, but Gelace's belly remained empty until Asna's tenth spring.

><-><-0-><-><

From the time of the last hawthorn blossom until the time of the first ramsons, Gelace's belly grew healthy-big and fruitful-ripe, and she and Eccet were whole-heart happy.

When the dog violets started to flower and sweet sap was leaking from the bark of the birch trees, Gelace took to her bed, ready to birth her new child. But she could not push the child out of her.

The child inside her stopped moving, and Gelace's body went lifeless limp, and her skin burned blistering hot with the fever. Convinced that his wife and unborn child would die, Eccet called Asna to his side to ready her for the grip of grief. But at that very moment, the door of their dwelling creaked open and a strange grey mist swirled its way inside. Out of the mist stepped a cloaked woman.

When she removed her hood, her long russet hair floated about her as if she were underwater. Her sage-green eyes held a season all of their own, and her skin shone brighter than the North Star.

'I am Dervla and I have come to help Gelace and the new

child,' said the stranger, her voice ringing sweeter than a drift of bluebells.

Eccet fancied that Dervla was no mortal and that he should be careful cautious of her, but he could feel the tender of her words and so he led her to where Gelace lay.

Dervla placed her hands on Gelace's belly and said, 'Bring me your sharpest sword, Eccet.'

Eccet was mighty worried by Dervla's request, but he fetched the sword quick-smart and gave it to her, and Dervla took the sword to Gelace's belly. The blade slicked through Gelace's flesh, and out of the wet wound clambered something so horrible hideous that it hurt Eccet's eyes to look at it.

The creature was no bigger than a man's hand and had the feary look of a pookah about it. It lopside-limped on all fours and its spine was crookit-curved. Its head was covered in thick black hair and its gums were planted with bright white teeth that were far too big for its mouth. Its skin was wrinkled and ragged-rough and bruised all black and blue. Its eyes wept bubbling blood and it howled like murder.

Dervla lifted the creature and kissed it and said, 'This is Amergin, son of Eccet and Gelace and brother of Asna. He will be loved.'

Dervla took Amergin to his father, and, as soon as Eccet took Amergin into his arms, his heart opened and took Amergin in. Eccet kissed his howling child and said, 'He will be loved.'

Asna reached up to touch her new brother, and, as soon as her fingers felt his skin, her heart opened and took Amergin in. Asna tickled her howling brother and said, 'He will be loved.'

Dervla magicked Gelace's belly closed and cooled the fever in her. Gelace opened her eyes, sat up and and said, 'Bring my son to me.'

Eccet took Amergin to his mother, and, as soon as Gelace took Amergin into her arms, her heart opened and took Amergin in. Gelace kissed her howling child and said, 'He will be loved.'

But Dervla was not done. She looked Eccet straight in the eye and said, 'And now I must take something.'

'You have saved my wife and my child, and my heart is bursting with a thousand thank yous. Of course, you must take something for your kindness! Take anything that pleases you, Dervla,' said Eccet, his voice full of big-plenty generous.

'I will take Amergin's voice,' said Dervla.

'Oh, Dervla! Have pity on the poor child!' cried Eccet. 'Will you not take something else? What about a sword so brave that it will win any battle? Or an axe so sharp that it will cut the sky and make it weep?'

'I will not take anything else. I will take Amergin's voice, but there is no need to fear. One day, I will return it,' answered Dervla, and Eccet looked deep into her sage-green eyes and saw that she was telling the truth.

Dervla bowed all reverent to Eccet, and then she lifted

Amergin out of Gelace's arms. Amergin continued to howl as Dervla kissed him and gentled him and cosied him and whispered strange stories in his ear.

After the stories were finished, Dervla put her mouth close to Amergin's and drew a long deep breath. As she breathed in, a wondrous brume drifted out of Amergin's mouth and into hers. The brume was all silver white and had the magick of moonlight about it.

When Dervla had taken in the full wonder of the brume, she closed her mouth tight and returned Amergin to Gelace. Amergin slipped into a peaceful slumber.

Without another word, Dervla lifted her hood over her head, turned herself into a grey mist and swirled her way out through the door.

Hazelnuts

It was not long before Amergin's hunger woke him. He stretched his jaws wide, his arms and legs wormed and wiggled, his eyes frothed and foamed with bubbling blood, but not a single sound came out of him.

Gelace's eyes filled with tears, her lips trembled and she said, 'While I am glad for my own life and for the life of my child, I am soul-sore sorry that I cannot hear my own son call for me. How long must we wait for the return of Amergin's voice, Eccet?'

'I do not know how long we must wait,' answered Eccet. 'Until Dervla returns, all we can do is love the poor boy and give him the best life we can.'

And for a full five years, that is exactly what they did: they loved Amergin and gave him the best life they could.

Gelace cosied and comforted him, Asna sang and rhymed to him, and Eccet sat him by the forge so that he was entertained by the spit-spattering of the sparks.

When people saw Amergin for the first time, they fair froze with the fright, but Eccet simply said, 'This is Amergin and he is my son and he will be loved. If you want your axe made fine or your sword made fair, you will bide a while and play with my boy.'

And that is exactly what people did. Eccet would give them a handful of hazelnuts in their shells, and they would sit on the floor opposite Amergin and roll the nuts to him, and Amergin would roll them right back. And then Amergin would smile a big-tooth smile and lopside-limp on all fours over to them, and they would pinch Amergin's ragged-rough cheeks and as soon as they touched his wrinkled skin, their hearts would open and let Amergin in.

On Amergin's fifth birthday, well before the sun was awake, the door of Eccet's dwelling creaked open and a strange grey mist swirled its way inside. Out of the mist stepped Dervla.

'I have brought a gift for Amergin,' she said.

Gelace's heart skipped and danced, the edges of her eyes creased with delight and she cried, 'At last! The day has come for Amergin's voice to be returned!'

'Oh no, Gelace,' said Dervla. 'I have not brought him his voice – I have brought him something *far* better. Now, where is Amergin?'

When Amergin heard his name, he lopside-leapt out of his favourite corner and sat at Dervla's feet. Dervla bent down and stretched out a clenched fist to him. As Amergin tried to prise her fist open, Dervla kissed him and gentled him and cosied him and whispered strange stories in his ear.

After the stories were finished, Dervla opened her fist. On her palm lay a single hazelnut in its shell. She sat down next to Amergin and rolled the nut to him and he rolled it right back. Then Dervla magicked the shell open and gave the nut to Amergin, and Amergin ate it.

'What a clever boy you are,' said Dervla.

Now, Eccet was quite clever himself, and even though he was disappointed by Dervla's pitiful gift, he knew better than to complain. So instead of mithering, Eccet bowed and said, 'How thoughtful of you, Dervla. There is nothing that pleases Amergin more than a hazelnut.'

Dervla smiled and said, 'I have been watching you all these past five years, and my gift is a reward for how well you have loved Amergin.'

Then Dervla lifted her hood over her head, turned herself into a grey mist and swirled her way out through the door.

><-><-0-<-><-<

When Dervla had gone, Eccet tumbled thoughts from one side of his head to the other, and after a while he said, 'If Dervla thinks that our love for Amergin is only worth a single hazelnut, then we must surely love the poor boy more.'

And, for another full year, that is exactly what they did: they loved Amergin more.

Gelace taught her son how to speak with his feelings instead of with words. When she cried, she put Amergin's hand to her chest and said, 'This is sadness and the ache of it is quiet and heavy and it speaks through my eyes.'

And then Amergin cried and Gelace knew that he had understood.

When Gelace laughed, she put Amergin's hand to her chest and said, 'This is joy and the burst of it is loud and light and it speaks at the edges of my mouth and the corners of my eyes.'

And then Amergin smiled and Gelace knew that he had understood.

By the end of the year, Amergin had learned how to grow

his feelings big enough for others to understand him, and he had learned how to understand people even when they were not talking.

⊱─━⊱⊰━─⊰

Asna took Amergin out on to the riverbank and into the fields and amused him with the noises of nature. She taught him how to recognise most every sound you could think of.

'Oh, Amergin!' she cried. 'Do you hear how the bees tickle their tongues in the syrup-sweet nectar?' And then she sang the song of the bees to Amergin and his ears opened wide and swallowed the sound, and his head bobbed along to the rhythm of it.

'Oh, Amergin!' she cried. 'Do you hear how the sycamore tells its children to fly?' And then she sang the song of the sycamore to Amergin and his ears opened wide and swallowed the sound, and his fingers fluttered like flying sycamore seeds.

By the end of the year, Amergin's ears had grown as clever as Asna's.

⊱─━⊱⊰━─⊰

Eccet set about teaching Amergin the secrets of a master smith.

'You must listen to the metal, Amergin – it knows what it wants to become,' he explained. 'It may look like I am forcing the shape of it, but, in truth, I am doing no such thing. The metal is telling me what I need to do to help it become what it wants to be – and I do as it bids.'

Before he took his hands to each new piece of metal, Eccet would play a game with his son. He would place the metal on the ground and call Amergin over to it. Amergin would look at the metal and smell it and put his hands and his feet and his ears to it. When the metal had told Amergin what it wanted to become, Amergin would draw the shape of an axe or a sword in the air and Eccet would smile at his son and say, 'That is exactly what it wants to become, and now I will do as it bids.'

And as Eccet hammered the metal with his fists and prettied it with his fingers, Amergin moved his hands about in the air as if he were crafting it too.

By the end of the year, Amergin understood each piece of metal as well as Eccet did.

The Rhyme

On Amergin's sixth birthday, well before the sun was awake,

the door of Eccet's dwelling creaked open and a strange grey mist swirled its way inside. Out of the mist stepped Dervla.

'I have brought a gift for Amergin,' said Dervla.

Gelace's heart skipped and danced and the edges of her eyes creased with delight. For the past year, Amergin had been loved so well that she was certain that Dervla would return the gift of speech to her son. Full of joy, she cried, 'At last! The day has come for Amergin's voice to be returned!'

'Oh no, Gelace,' said Dervla. 'I have not brought him his voice – I have brought him something *far* better. Where is Amergin?'

When Amergin heard his name, he lopside-leapt out of his favourite corner and sat at Dervla's feet, just as he had before. Dervla bent down and stretched out a clenched fist to him. As Amergin tried to prise her fist open, Dervla kissed him and gentled him and cosied him and whispered strange stories in his ear, just as she had before.

After the stories were finished, Dervla opened her fist. On her palm lay a single hazelnut in its shell. She sat down next to Amergin and rolled the nut to him and he rolled it right back. Then Dervla magicked the shell open and gave the nut to Amergin, and Amergin ate it.

'What a clever boy you are,' said Dervla, just as she had before.

Now, Eccet wanted to rage and fury at Dervla for her pitiful gift, but he knew that if he was ungracious, she might never return his son's voice. So he cooled his temper and bowed and said, 'How thoughtful of you, Dervla. There is nothing that pleases Amergin more than a hazelnut.'

Dervla smiled and said, 'I have been watching you all this past year, and my gift is a reward for how well you have loved Amergin.'

Then Dervla lifted her hood over her head, turned herself into a grey mist and swirled her way out through the door.

⊱──━━─◦○◦─━━──⊰

When Dervla had gone, Gelace's eyes puddled with tears and she cried, 'But there is no son better loved than ours!'

Asna put her voice into the saddest key and sang, 'But there is no brother better loved than mine!'

Eccet tumbled thoughts from one side of his head to the other, and after a while he said, 'If Dervla thinks that our love for Amergin is still only worth a single hazelnut, then we must surely love the poor boy more.'

'But how can we love him more?' asked Gelace.

'We will have to learn new ways,' answered Eccet.

⊱──━━─◦○◦─━━──⊰

And that is exactly what they did: they learned new ways to love Amergin.

Gelace told Amergin every story she knew and when she ran out of stories, she made him new ones. She decorated the stories with most every feeling you could imagine, and Amergin smiled and wept and hoped and feared and felt the full of them all.

Asna grew into a woman, married a farmer and had a child of her own. She brought the child to Amergin and Amergin cosied and gentled it and rolled hazelnuts in their shells to it, and the child opened its heart and let Amergin in.

Eccet told Amergin the secrets of living and dying and loved his son into a young man.

But, no matter how well they loved him, for the next seven years Dervla brought the same gift to Amergin: a single hazelnut in its shell.

⊱━━⊱⟐⊰━━⊰

On Amergin's fourteenth birthday, well before the sun was awake, the door of Eccet's dwelling creaked open and a strange grey mist swirled its way in. Out of the mist stepped Dervla.

'I have brought a gift for Amergin,' said Dervla.

Gelace's heart did not skip and dance when she saw Dervla. Readying herself for the usual gift, Gelace softened the sharp edges of her words as best she could and said, 'Have you brought Amergin a hazelnut? There is nothing that pleases him more than a hazelnut, Dervla.'

'Oh no, Gelace,' said Dervla. 'I have not brought him a hazelnut – I have brought him something *far* better. Where is Amergin?'

When Amergin heard his name, he lopside-leapt out of his favourite corner and sat at Dervla's feet, just as he had done nine times before.

Since his fifth birthday, Amergin had not stretched an inch in length, nor had he managed to lift himself upright. The crookit-curve of his back tightened by the day, and, no matter how often Gelace wiped his face, it was always smeared with rills of bubbling blood. His ragged-rough skin was so sore that he could not bear the pain of clothes, and, in spite of a meagre diet of nuts and curds, he had the bulbous belly of a toad.

Amergin smiled at Dervla and his enormous white teeth fair filled the room. Dervla lifted Amergin into her arms and drew his face nose-close to hers. She tidied his mop of matted black hair and said, 'Now, Amergin, close your eyes as tight as I used to clench my fists when I brought you the hazelnuts.'

Amergin did as he was told, and Eccet and Gelace watched wordless as Dervla opened her mouth and let a wondrous, silvery-white brume drift out of her mouth and into Amergin's.

Just as the last of the brume disappeared into Amergin's

mouth, there was a knock at the door and a man walked in. The man was called Greth and he was the servant of Athirne, the chief bard of Ulster and poet to the great king, Conchobar mac Nessa. Greth had visited Eccet's forge many times before and he too had rolled many a hazelnut to Amergin and opened his heart and let the boy in.

Greth was in such a hurry that he did not even notice Dervla. 'My master is in urgent need of another fine axe from you, Eccet,' he said. 'If I return in three days, can you have it ready?'

Eccet nodded his head and opened his mouth to reply, but before he could speak a single word, Amergin leapt out of Dervla's arms. Full of pleased-to-see-you, he lopside-limped towards Greth and, with a voice that was fair jumping with joy, he said:

> Will gentle Greth stay a while if his time be free?
> Will he roll a nut or two? Will Greth eat curds with me?

As soon as the words were out of Amergin's mouth, a strange grey mist swirled its way all about him and disappeared him in a thick choke of fog. Out of the fog stepped a young man, and it is no bend of the truth to say that he was the most handsome young man that ever got made.

His brow was strong and his jaw was well cut. His back was broad and firm, and if you had taken a plumb-bob to it, you would have found nothing straighter. He was healthy tall and work-hard slender, and his eyes shone as blue and as lively as a pair of young spring gentians. His black hair curled around his neck and tumbled on to his shoulders, and his smile was honest and true. Dressed like a nobleman from a faraway place, he wore a coat threaded with most every colour you could imagine.

Greth could not speak: he was astonished at Amergin's words and skilful rhymery.

Eccet could not speak: he was magicked by the look of the handsome young man.

But Gelace *could* speak: the angry hurt boiled out of her and she said, 'Where is my son, Dervla? Have you not done enough harm? You took our son's voice, you have insulted us with paltry gifts for the last nine years, and now you have taken our poor boy from us and put a stranger in his place. What cruelty is this?'

Dervla did not speak, but the handsome young man did. He looked Gelace in the eye and said, 'I am no stranger, Mother. I am Amergin.'

The Faerie Poet

Eccet and Gelace humbled themselves into a deep bow

and thanked Dervla. They were rapturous happy at the return of Amergin's voice and the healthy new shape of his body.

'Bring out our best meat and our finest cheese, Gelace! Let our guests join us for a breakfast feast and let us celebrate the fourteenth birthday of Amergin,' cried Eccet, his feet shuffling a jig of joy and his hands clapping along in time.

⊶─◆─○─◆─⊷

Eccet, Gelace, Amergin, Dervla and Greth sat around the fire. They filled their bellies with food and sweetened the air with good feelings and took it in turns to tell Amergin's story.

'This is the story of Amergin,' began Gelace. 'There was once a child who was cut out of his mother's belly.'

Amergin grinned and everyone else cried, 'And may Amergin's story be told a thousand times!'

Gelace turned to Eccet.

'This is the story of Amergin,' began Eccet. 'There was once a child who could speak without talking. His ears were keener than a hound's, and he knew all the secrets of a master smith.'

Amergin grinned and everyone else cried, 'And may Amergin's story be told a thousand times!'

Eccet turned to Greth.

'This is the story of Amergin,' began Greth. 'There was

once a child who always warm-welcomed a guest, no matter how lowly his standing, and who liked rolling hazelnuts.'

Amergin grinned and everyone else cried, 'And may Amergin's story be told a thousand times!'

Greth turned to Dervla.

'This is the story of Amergin,' began Dervla. 'There was once a child who called for help at its birthing time. The child said that it was not made for living and that it would soon die. The child said that if it was not taken from its mother's belly, then its dead body would poison its mother and she would die too. The child asked for its mother to be saved.'

Dervla did not short-story it as the others had done. Instead, Dervla told the full of it, and this is what she said.

'A faerie heard the child's call, and it was the saddest and sweetest mortal voice that she had ever heard. The faerie told her father about the child's sad, sweet voice and its call for help, and her father told her to answer the call. He said that the child was so noble that it should not only be made good for living, but that it should also be well rewarded. Her father told her to bring the child's voice to him after it was born.

'The faerie saved the mother and made the child good for living. And then the faerie took the child's voice to her father. Her father was Bardán, the greatest of the faerie poets. Bardán was so skilled that he crafted the call of the curlew, wrote the rhythm of the rain and sonneted the sound of the River Bush.

Bardán rewarded the child by teaching its voice the ways of faerie poetry.

'For fourteen years, Bardán trained the voice of the child, and for fourteen years, Bardán's daughter watched how well the child was loved by its mortal family. There was no child better loved. Bardán's daughter could see that the child's parents heart-ached for the return of their child's voice, but it was not ready to leave the care of the faerie poet. Instead, she rewarded their love as best she could.

'She went to a place called the Well of Wisdom. Around the well grew nine hazels, and in the well grew a great salmon. That salmon ate a single nut from each of the trees, and when it had eaten nine nuts, the salmon knew everything that there was to know and became the Salmon of Knowledge. Bardán's daughter took a nut from each of those hazels and gave them to the child. When the child had eaten the last of the nine nuts, it too knew everything that there was to know – just like the salmon.

'When the child's voice was almost fourteen years old, it turned into a man's voice. Bardán had taught it so well that any faerie would have taken it for the voice of the poet himself. Only then did Bardán tell his daughter to return the voice to its owner, which she did.

'On the child's fourteenth birthday, the faerie took the voice to the child's dwelling. Although the child's body had not grown, she could see that he had been loved into a young man. The faerie blew the voice back into the young man. And, as soon as the young man spoke, the magick of his own voice made his body healthy.'

━►━┥◆┝━○━┥◆┝━◄

When Dervla finished speaking, the only sound to be heard was the crickle-crackle of the fire. Gelace took Dervla's hands in hers and kissed them. Eccet's eyes streamed with a thousand thank yous.

Amergin bowed all reverent to Dervla, and she smiled at him, stroked his cheek and warm-whispered, 'And may Amergin's story be told a thousand times!'

Then Greth stood up, his face painted bright with gladness and his heart brimming with the goodness of it all. He said, 'I must go to straight to my master and tell him the wondrous story of Amergin. I'd wager my horse that as soon as he hears it, the words will rise up in him like a mighty torrent and a great poem will be written!'

Athirne

Greth jumped up on to his horse and hurtled home to his

master, Athirne. Without delay, Greth told Athirne the story of Amergin.

He told Athirne how Amergin's first words had been a clever rhyme. He told Athirne how Amergin had walked all straight-backed and handsome out of a magick mist. He told Athirne how Amergin had become as wise as the Salmon of Knowledge and how his voice had been trained by Bardán, the greatest of the faerie poets.

When Greth had finished telling the story of Amergin, he said, 'Is this not wondrous news? Do the words of a great poem rise up in you, Master?'

'Indeed, my heart bursts with joy to hear this wondrous news, Greth!' said Athirne. 'A magnificent poem about Amergin already moves and grows in me, but I must see the young man for myself before I compose it. There is no need for you to collect my axe from Eccet – I will go to him myself. I know how well you love Amergin, and I'm sure that, as soon as I see him with my own eyes, my heart will open and let him in just as yours did. My love for Amergin will inspire the greatest poem I have ever written!' Athirne smiled a smile so warm that it would have burned you if you had been standing too close to it.

But it was not a real smile.

In truth, Athirne did not like this news at all. He was frantic fearful that Amergin might steal his place as the chief bard of Ulster and poet to the great king, Conchobar mac Nessa.

Athirne had no intention of writing a poem about Amergin, but he had every intention of killing him.

▷─◆▷─○─◁◆─◁

When the day came to collect his axe, Athirne saddled his fastest horse and set out for Eccet's forge. Athirne had devised a cunning plan and was so proud of it that he rhymed to the rhythm of his horse's gallop as he rode:

> *The seeds of my fate on this day will be sown:*
> *a poor young poet will be cut to the bone!*
> *My place will be safe in the heart of the king*
> *when I slice up the faerie-mouthed Amergin!*

Faster and faster galloped the horse, and over and over rhymed Athirne. He rhymed to the river, he rhymed to the wind and he rhymed to a robin: beak, breast and wing.

Now, the robin understood the rhyme and did not like it. The robin carried the rhyme to Dervla and sang it to her, and she did not like it either.

Dervla quick-misted herself to Eccet's dwelling and told him that Athirne was coming to kill Amergin. She told Gelace to take Amergin to his sister's farm and hide him there. She told Eccet to go to the riverbank, dig up seven shovels of clay and take them to the forge.

When the clay was all heaped up, Dervla told Eccet to use

his clever hands to form the clay into a likeness of Amergin. Eccet worked miracle-fast, and, as soon as he had finished, Dervla whispered magick words into the clay figure's mouth. The figure started to breathe and its clay flesh rosied up, but it did not stir or open its eyes. It looked just like it was sleeping.

Dervla told Eccet to move the likeness of Amergin into a corner and cosy a blanket over it.

'Now you are ready for Athirne,' smiled Dervla. 'Let him think that he has killed your son, and all will be well.'

Dervla lifted her hood over her head, turned herself into a grey mist and fast-swirled her way out through the door.

>─+◆>─0─<◆+─<

When Athirne arrived at the forge, he bowed to Eccet and said, 'I am Athirne, chief bard of Ulster and poet to the great king, Conchobar mac Nessa. You have made three fine axes for me and three fine swords, and no better weapons have I ever seen. I have come today not only to collect my new axe, but also to offer my personal thanks for your craftsmanship.'

Eccet bowed back and said, 'I am honoured to welcome such a great man to my forge.' Then he pointed to the blanketed figure in the corner and said, 'Please forgive me for not introducing you to my son, but he is so in need of restful sleep that I dare not wake him.'

'Oh, let the boy sleep!' insisted Athirne, stretching a smile a furlong wide.

Eccet gave the axe to Athirne and said, 'May this new axe reward you a thousand times over!'

Athirne marvelled at the beauty of it. Nothing in nature was as well shaped or as finely decorated. When he swung it, the glitter of it was blind-a-man bright and the sharp of it made the air scream.

'I'd wager that it's the best axe I've ever made,' said Eccet.

Although Athirne was in full agreement with Eccet, he shook his head, sorrowful-sighed and said, 'I am rather disappointed with this axe, Eccet. Have you nothing else to show me?'

Now, Eccet had nothing else to show Athirne, but he was clever enough to read the wiley of the bard's request and said, 'I may indeed have something else to show you. Please excuse me while I go and look for it.'

Eccet bowed again and then left the forge, but he did not go very far. He hid in the bushes just outside the opening of the forge and watched as Athirne raised the new axe high in the air and brought it down hard into the clay likeness of Amergin.

Over and over, Athirne raised the axe high and brought it down hard, chopping the clay likeness into five chunks. Then he carved and he cut and he sliced and he cleft and he chopped and he minced until nothing was left.

When Athirne was so spent that he could no longer raise his axe, he staggered out of the forge, hauled himself on to his horse and urged the animal to hurry him home.

When Athirne was a field away from home, he met Greth.

Greth was stifled with swelter and soused with sweat and had run the breath fair out of himself. All popping with panic, he panted, 'The great king, Conchobar mac Nessa, waits for you.'

The Bard of Ulster

When Athirne arrived at his dwelling, he scurried inside and flung himself at the feet of the great king, Conchobar mac Nessa.

'My lord, my king, great warrior and generous patron of the arts,' fawned Athirne, 'so honoured am I by your unexpected visit to my humble dwelling that the words already move in me to write my greatest poem yet!'

'This visit will leave no mark of honour on your house, poet!' thundered the king. 'Today I was visited by Dervla, daughter of Bardán, the greatest of the faerie poets.

'Dervla told me the story of Amergin. She told me about his noble spirit. She told me how her father had trained Amergin's voice and how Amergin had become as wise as the Salmon of Knowledge. She told me how Amergin's mother had taught him to speak with feelings instead of words, and how his sister had taught his ears to honour the beauty of sound, and how his father had taught him the secret of crafting and shaping things. She told me that there was no man who would make a greater bard of Ulster, or poet to the king, than Amergin mac Eccit.'

Athirne's face blanched. His heart thumped against his ribs. He said nothing.

'Then Dervla told me how you rode to Eccet's forge and how you raised your axe high and brought it down hard,' the king said, all stern and steady.

Athirne dropped to his knees and cried, 'Have mercy on me, oh gracious king! It is true that I killed Amergin. I did not want to lose my place in your heart, but now I fear that I have. Tell me how I may win it back!'

After a very long pause, the king continued, 'And then Dervla told me about a robin who heard you rhyming. She told me how the robin took the rhyme to her and how she took the rhyme to Eccet's forge and how Eccet shaped a likeness of his son out of clay and how Dervla magicked it to look real.'

Athirne opened his mouth but no words came out.

'Amergin is alive, Athirne, and if you want to keep a place in my heart, you must take him as your apprentice and teach him everything you know. Train him for a thousand days, and I will forgive you for what you have done.'

>-<>-○-<>-<

And that is exactly what Athirne did: he trained Amergin for a thousand days and taught him everything he knew.

Athirne taught Amergin great poems from faraway places. He taught him a thousand new words and how to off-by-heart most any story you could think of. He taught him how to big-speak a poem so that the words would fill a feasting hall and shake the bones of its walls.

After a thousand days, Amergin knew everything that Athirne knew, and Athirne woke up to find that his voice had left him. The king forgave him and allowed him keep a place in his heart, but from that day on, Athirne never spoke again. Amergin became the chief bard of Ulster and poet to the great king, Conchobar mac Nessa, and whenever Amergin performed a poem, the hearts of those who listened to him opened and took him in. There was no poet in Ulster who was better loved than Amergin.

In time, Amergin became not only a great poet, but also a great warrior. He killed a three-headed monster called the Ellén Trechend and stopped an entire army in its tracks by throwing stones at it. He married Findchóem, sister of the great king, Conchobar mac Nessa, and together they had a son called Conall Cernach, and he too grew into a great warrior. Amergin and Findchóem also raised a boy who was not their own. The boy was called Sétanta and he grew into a man known as Cú Chulainn. And the deeds of Cú Chulainn were so great that they are still memoried by poets today.

And this is the story of Amergin. May his story be told a thousand times!

The MERROW of MURLOUGH BAY

The Soul Cages

In the deepest, darkest, most dangerous current, in the waters between Murlough Bay and the Mull of Kintyre, lived the mightiest merrows that ever swam the seas. The current was called The Big Deep, and most every walking man was afraid of it.

The merrowmaids in The Big Deep wore fishtails that could outshine the blue of any mackerel. They were gifted with voices that could charm a walking man's heart so wide open that it would never close. They had the mystery of the ocean in their soothing, green eyes and an eternal summer in every waterfall of their glistening, golden hair. There was nothing more beautiful in the sea, on the land or in the skies than the merrowmaids who lived in The Big Deep, in the waters between Murlough Bay and the Mull of Kintyre.

But the merrowmen weren't beautiful at all. They wore slimy, brown fishtails and had barely-there, burning-red eyes that were so close together you'd go cross-eyed if you looked at them. They had sharp, muddy-green teeth that lazy-leaned in all different directions. They had tangled-seaweed hair and snouts that any pig would be proud of. There was nothing uglier in the sea, on the land or in the skies than the merrowmen who lived in The Big Deep, in the waters between Murlough Bay and the Mull of Kintyre.

Because the merrowmen were so ugly, the merrowmaids tried as hard as they could to get themselves stolen from the sea by the walking men. When the sea was calm, they laid themselves out on the rocks closest to the sea so that the walking men could wade out to them, and when the wind was still, they sang their best songs so that the walking men were enchanted by them. The merrowmaids tried as hard as they could to marry a walking man so that they did not have to marry a merrowman.

The merrowmaids soft-butter-heart-loved the walking men, but the merrowmen hated them. They hated them for stealing their women from the sea. They hated them because even those merrowmaids who did not get stolen from the sea only took a merrowman for a husband to get with child. If a merrowmaid took a merrowman for a husband, she would not let him feel the spring-tide waves of her heart. Instead, she would scorn him and small him right down, and then, as soon as she had her merrowchild, she would leave him.

▷—◁▷—○—◁▷—◁

One big autumn tide, the merrowmen got so raged up that they decided to start stealing the walking men and salt-wound-punishing them for taking the merrowmaids from the sea.

In the beginning, they stole just a few of the walking men at a time. They waited for the fishermen to go out in their tiddler boats, then they turned off the light in the sky and scary-swirled up the waters between Murlough Bay and the Mull of Kintyre.

The merrowmen turned the tiddler boats upside down, dragged the walking men into the sea and pushed the water into their lungs until their eyes bulged. Then, once the flailing limbs of the walking men had stopped fighting, the merrowmen ripped out their human souls and locked them in soul cages chained to the bottom of the sea. The cages were guarded by young merrowmen who prodded the sorry souls with rusty tridents and allowed them no rest.

The merrowmen tangled up the bodies of the no-longer-walking men in the beds of seaweed, and, when they were all rotted down, they hauled the bodies up on to the sea and waited to hear the big hurting tears of the still-walking men who found them.

But, after a while, the merrowmen weren't satisfied with wrecking the tiddler boats of the fishermen in that narrow stretch of water. They started to scary-swirl up the water around Rathlin, Islay and Jura – and beyond. After a while, the merrowmen started to wreck big ships. After a while, they started to wreck whole armadas.

>-+-•-•-•-◦-‹•›-‹

The people with the old magick in their blood say that there was only ever one someone who tried to stop the merrowmen from stealing the walking men's souls. But the truth of it is that it wasn't really a someone who tried to stop them. It was a merrowman.

Not many of the people with the old magick in their blood will speak of what happened. They say that the story is so feary grim that it hurts to tell it, and it hurts to hear it.

But I have heard it. And I will tell it to you.

I cannot say that it will not hurt me to tell you this story. I cannot say that it will not hurt you to hear it. But I can say that, if you open your ears wide enough, this is a story that will not only grow your heart bigger, softer and braver – it will also grow your head wiser.

Bright Blue

One ferocious winter tide, after a mighty big wrecking, the merrowmen from The Big Deep dragged their bounty down to the bottom of the sea. They had made a fine catch: at least forty more human souls were squeezed into the bulging cages that night. There were thousands of souls trapped in those cages, all howling like injured dogs. The band of marauding merrowmen had good reason to celebrate.

'This calls for a gallon or five of dulse ale,' bellowed Slap, as he puffed up his merrow lungs with great pride. 'Which of you young-tails is guardin' tonight?'

The young merrowmen cast down their barely-there eyes in the hope of avoiding the duty. The feasting would be second to none in The Big Deep that night, and most all of those young-tails were kipping keen to join the celebrations.

Only Bright Blue lifted his trident. 'I will happily do the guarding tonight.'

'Well, young-tail, you make sure that if them stinkin' souls quieten down, you prod 'em an' poke 'em real good. If that human soul-howlin' can't be heard above our hollerin' an' whip-tailin', well, I'll be down to prod an' poke you, my lad.'

All the other merrowmen scare-sniggered at Slap's words, but Bright Blue knew exactly what to do. Bright Blue *grrrrrd* and shook his rusty trident at the soul cages to reassure Slap.

Satisfied, Slap pointed his trident towards The Big Deep, and in the swish of a tail all the merrowmen were gone, leaving Bright Blue on his own.

After no time at all, Bright Blue could hear drunken celebrating coming from The Big Deep. It was a filthy, loud sound. He knew it was time to get to work. But Bright Blue would not be guarding the cages or prodding the cages or poking the cages. Instead, Bright Blue would be opening the cages.

Bright Blue was not like the other merrowmen, old or young. He had grown his heart big enough to feel a deep, dirty shame for stealing the souls of the walking men. He had grown his heart soft enough to feel sorry for them, even though they stole the merrowmaids out of the sea. He had grown his heart brave enough to free the human souls from the cages. And he had grown his head wise enough to know that, when he freed the human souls, he would have to leave The Big Deep for ever. If the merrowmen from The Big Deep ever netted him for his crime, then his punishment would be The Worst Thing.

><><-O-<><><

Bright Blue swam in amongst the cages. The human souls were in so much pain that their howls almost reached the roof of the sea. It was the kind of sound that would fill up your ears and heavy your heart right out of the bottom of your feet.

Bright Blue raised himself to his full height, filled his powerful merrow lungs and blew out a torpedo of bubbles. The soul cages quietened and he began to speak to them.

'I know that you are condemned to suffer for all eternity as long as you are trapped in the soul cages. My own soul hurts to listen to you, and I am sore-sorry that we pushed water into your lungs and rotted down your human bodies in the seaweed. I will free you so that you may find your final resting place – whether that resting place is the Above-the-Sky place or the Below-the-Sea place – but you must help me. If Slap cannot hear your wailing, he will fast-tail it down here, and we will all be in trouble that is even deeper than The Big Deep.'

As soon as Bright Blue had finished speaking, the soul cages started to shake, the bottom of the ocean started to tremble, and the most soul-ripping sound that had ever been made tore through the water, right from the bottom of the sea to the top of it.

Bright Blue worked as fast as he could to open the soul cages. If he saw souls floating upwards, he used his tail to whip them up into the Above-the-Sky place. If he saw souls floating downwards, he used his tail to slap them down into the Below-the-Sea place. And, as he worked, the souls continued to help the merrow by making the soul-ripping sound, even when they had reached their resting place.

Bright Blue was just opening the last cage when he felt the ripple of more than a hundred merrows fast-tailing it down to the soul cages. Even though his cold fish-blood started to freeze with fear, he kept on working. He kept whipping up the floating souls and slapping down the sinking souls.

But he should have stopped working. He should have left that last cage. He should have whip-tailed it away from there as fast as he could, because what happened next was The Worst Thing.

The Worst Thing

Slap's one good eye nearly popped out of his head when he saw Bright Blue helping the last of the walking men's souls to their resting place.

'What is this treachery?' boomed the old merrowman as he looked around at the empty cages. 'An' to think that I was comin' to congratulate you on all that soul-howlin'. To think that I was bringin' you a keg of ale to soak yoursel' in. To think that I didn't want you to be missin' out on our celebratin'.'

Bright Blue brave-eyed Slap.

All the merrowmen were ugly, but Slap was the ugliest of them all. He was the kind of ugly that would make you heave up your belly bile – and keep on heaving even when there was nothing left. He was five hundred years old and his salt-dried face bore a barnacle for every year he'd lived. He'd lost an eye to a fishing hook, and he'd blunted his sharp, muddy-green teeth by chewing off the hulls of too many galleons.

But although Slap was old, he was big-wave powerful. There wasn't a living creature under the sea that wasn't feary'd of his mighty, slapping tail.

'Don't you look at me all brave-eyed, pretty boy. Explain yoursel'!' hissed Slap.

Once again, Bright Blue raised himself to his full height. He was as tall as a main mast and looked down on most every merrowman, including Slap. His top-half was merrowman-ugly, but his bottom-half was merrowmaid-fine – instead of the slimy, brown fishtail worn by most merrowmen, Bright Blue wore a handsome, bluer-than-a-mackerel one. He was no more than one hundred years old, but though he was young, Bright Blue was lone-shark brave.

'It is wrong that we keep stealing the souls of the walking men. It is wrong that we keep tangling up their bodies in seaweed and rotting them down. It is wrong that we do not let the souls of the walking men go to their resting place – whether that resting place is the Above-the-Sky place or the Below-the-Sea place. I have opened the soul cages because our own souls will shrivel if we continue to salt-wound-punish those poor walking men. They do not deserve this.' As he spoke, he brave-eyed Slap and all the other merrowmen that hovered behind him, and his fishtail did not quiver once.

Slap started pounding his fishtail on the floor of the sea, slowly and rhythmically. A hundred merrow fishtails began to pound to the same rhythm.

'Young-tail, you soft-talk like a merrowmaid,' Slap declared. 'It is clear to all of us that you soft-butter-heart-love the walkin' men – this love is foolish an' misplaced, but you must learn this for yoursel'. Your punishment for freein' the human souls will be The Worst Thing. We will cut off your pretty-boy tail, turn you into a walkin' man and banish you to the land. You will soon see that those walkin' men are much crueller than us merrowmen. I wager my own tail that those walkin' sludge-for-souls will put you in a cage before the year is out.'

⊳—⊷—O—⊷—⊲

After Slap's judgement, the merrowmen took Bright Blue to the lobsters. The lobsters sheared off Bright Blue's bluer-than-a-mackerel tail with their clippety claws, leaving only a narrow thread of blue around his waist. From old, barnacled boat timbers the merrowmen nailed together two uneven legs. Then they found an odd pair of rotting walking men's feet, and the lobsters used rusty fishhooks to attach the putrid feet to the timbers.

Once that was done, the lobsters took the tops of the timber legs and whittled them to draw-your-blood points. The lobsters shoved the pointy tops of the legs squelch-hard up into Bright Blue's wound and tarred the joints water-tight.

Then the merrowmen tail-slapped Bright Blue right out of the water and on to the beach at Murlough Bay, where he landed, directly below the hill at Benvan.

Malock

After the dizziness had gone, Bright Blue tried to stand up on his new legs, but the pain was so poker-hot that he couldn't. So he rolled on to his front and used his elbows and his forearms to drag himself away from the water's edge. The skin on his elbows and forearms tore and bled, his rotting feet snagged on every rock and shell, and each time his bottom half caught up with his top half, the tops of his new legs sliced into his insides like a pair of unskilled butchers. But, in spite of his torture, Bright Blue kept moving. He didn't stay still for longer than a sigh.

After a good painful while, Bright Blue found himself at the top of a grassy slope next to a ruined church. He thought that he would be safe there because it looked like the walking men had forgotten this holy place. Grass crept right over the crumbled-down walls, and the stones to mark the bones of the dead people had been scoured blank by the salty wind.

Next to the ruins of the church was a cave. Bright Blue hauled himself into the mouth of the cave and managed to prop himself up against a boulder. He looked out across the ruins and into the icy winter night, and he started to cry.

At first, he only cried tears the size of a raindrop. These tears were for the loss of his tail. Then he cried tears the size of a puddle. These tears were for the pain of his new legs.

Then he cried tears the size of a pond. These tears were for the walking men who would continue to have their souls put into cages by Slap and the other merrowmen.

And just as he started to cry tears the size of a lough, Bright Blue heard coughing and spluttering coming from outside the cave. He leaned forward as best he could and saw a full set of bones sit right up out of the muddy ground. But before Bright Blue had time to get scared, the bones started to speak.

'Who is trying to drown me in my sleep?' ached the bones.

'Oh, I am sorry for my tears, and I am sorry to disturb you. I was just taking shelter from the cold winter night,' Bright Blue said, and he started to cry again.

'Why are you crying tears the size of a lough?' asked the bones, wiping mud from its eye sockets with handfuls of frosty grass.

'These tears are for my all-on-my-ownness,' sobbed Bright Blue.

But Bright Blue's sobbing was soon interrupted. When its eye sockets were finally clear, the bones spied the full ugly of the merrow and sicked up a whole slide of mud.

'Are you not well?' enquired Bright Blue.

'You have a rather … unusual look about you,' said the bones.

'As do you,' retorted Bright Blue, his tears beginning to dry.

'Will you tell me the story of who you really are?' asked the bones.

Bright Blue did as he was asked and told the bones the big black of it all. He told the bones about the merrowmen of The Big Deep and how they pushed water into the lungs of walking men and ripped out their souls. He told the bones about the soul cages and how he came to lose his tail. He told the bones how his legs and feet got made – and how he could not walk for the hurt of it. He told the bones how he came to be slapped up on to the beach at Murlough Bay.

The bones soaked up every drop of the story and creaked with the pain of it. When Bright Blue had finished his story, he asked to hear the story of the bones.

'I am Malock,' the bones said, 'and I am the holy man that built this church. I was so good at the holying that, when I died, they sainted me up. When the time came to go to the Above-the-Sky place, I asked to sleep down here with my church by the sea, and so they put a bit of the Above-the-Sky place right down here – in my bed.'

Bright Blue was magicked by Malock's story and thanked him for telling it.

'Bright Blue, I must thank you for opening the cages and guiding the souls to their resting places. I want to give you three gifts in return for helping the walking men,' said Malock in a saint-soft voice.

'My first gift to you is something for your new legs and feet.

For as long as you want, you may lift clay from my bed and slop-slather it on to your body. The clay is full of holy, and it will soothe your poker-hot pain.

'My second gift to you is the cave next to my bed. The cave rests on sacred ground. You will always be safe here, and I will be glad of your good company.

'My third gift to you is the promise of the sweetest, deepest final sleep. When the time comes for you to stay in the Big Long Dream, you will have nothing to fear.'

Bright Blue thanked Malock for his generous gifts. Malock lay down into the ground and went back to sleep.

Bright Blue took a handful of the holy clay and rubbed it on to the bits of him that hurt him the most – the soles of his rotting feet, his fish-hook-torn ankles and the tar joint at his waist. The clay soothed the hot hurt and cooled it all down.

Bright Blue stood up and walked his new legs down to the sea. He waded into the water up to his tar-joint waist, scooped out a breakfast of pollock and returned to the cave. He filled up his belly and watched the day yawn itself awake.

The Beautiful Belong

A bulge of tides came and went. Bright Blue spent his days

watching the tiddler boats of the fishermen from his cave, and he was heart-pleased for them when they returned safely to sea with full nets. At night, when the burn came, he covered himself in Malock's clay and yarned with the bones of the holy man until the sea sang them both to sleep.

Bright Blue was glad of Malock's company in the evenings, but, as the tides passed, his all-on-my-ownness grew bigger and bigger.

One day, just after the snowdrops came, Bright Blue could not bear the lonely of it any longer. He watched the fishermen from his cave as usual. He watched them heave their nets ashore and, as soon as they started their slow, homeward plod up through the larches and sycamores, Bright Blue braved himself out of his cave so that he could follow them. He dared himself dangerous-close to them so that he could hear their laughing and feel the warmth between them. He hobbled behind them as quickly as he could, keeping himself hidden in the shadows.

By the time the fishermen were halfway up the hill, the sky had darkened. The walking men took leave of each other and went in the direction of their own homes.

Bright Blue decided to follow the fisherman with the kindest eyes. After no time at all, the fisherman opened the door of a tiny cottage and went inside.

Bright Blue pressed his snout against a cracked window and saw candles burning inside. He saw the fisherman's wife warm-

hold her husband's face. He saw the fisherman dry out his feet by a peat fire while his wife cooked his supper. And in a corner, sitting on the stone floor, Bright Blue saw a little boy. The little boy was busy playing with an old wooden spinning top.

When the supper was cooked, the fisherman's wife put the pan on the table and shouted over to the little boy. The little boy did not move. The fisherman went to his wife and put his arms around her. Bright Blue could see her crying.

'Why do you call him when he cannot hear?' asked the fisherman.

'The fever may have burned out his ears, but I pray every day that he will hear the sweetness and sourness of the world once again,' answered his wife. 'I call him in the hope that today is the day that my prayers have been answered.'

When Bright Blue heard the words of the fisherman's wife, the hurt of them went straight to his eyes and the heavy of them went straight to his heart.

The fisherman stroked the little boy's black hair to get his attention and then pointed to the table. The little boy had the same kindness in his eyes as his father, and Bright Blue watched how the fisherman and his wife cosied the little boy and spoke to him without speaking.

After they had finished eating, the fisherman tucked his little boy into his little bed. When the candles had burned right down, the fisherman and his wife got into their big bed and fell asleep.

Although the burn was already starting in his legs, Bright Blue waited. As soon as the cottage was all quiet, he hobbled silently through the door and over to the little boy's bed. Then he carefully took the hearing from his best ear and shared it between the two ears of the little boy.

The little boy stirred and opened his eyes, but it was too dark for him to see anything. Bright Blue tried as best he could to tiptoe away on his rotting feet, but the little boy heard him moving. He jumped out of his bed and cried at the top of his voice, 'My ears are working! My ears are working!'

Bright Blue pressed himself into the darkest corner he could find. The fisherman and his wife jumped out of bed. The fisherman lit a candle, and his wife embraced her son and cried and laughed at the same time. But as the candle's light danced into the corners of the cottage, the fisherman's wife screamed. 'Husband, there is a monster in our house!'

The little boy, the fisherman and the fisherman's wife all jumped on to the big bed in fright. They were so fearied of the merrow that the sick that was on its way up from their bellies stuck in their gullets. Bright Blue was sorry to have frightened them. He had hoped to leave without them noticing, and now the fright was settling into him too.

'I meant you no harm,' he said. 'I just wanted to help your little boy. My ears can hear better than any dolphin's, and I have plenty of hearing to spare. The hearing I have given to your son will last him his whole life. Even in old age, he will be able to hear the sound of the dawn rising, he will be able to hear the kick of a child in its mother's womb before she can feel it, and he will be able to hear the peaceful sighs of your souls when they go to the Above-the-Sky place.'

The fisherman's wife leapt off the big bed and warm-held the face of Bright Blue, just as she had warm-held the face of her husband earlier, and Bright Blue's heart glowed big inside him. The fisherman and his wife gave him a basket full of cheese, honey and bread, and the little boy stood at the door of the cottage and waved the merrow back into the night.

<hr />

As soon as Bright Blue arrived back at the cave, Malock awoke and sat up from the ground. As Bright Blue slop-slathered the clay on to the bits of him that hurt the most, he told the holy man about the fisherman and his wife and the little boy who could not hear. As he shared the cheese, honey and bread with the hungry bones of the holy man, Bright Blue told him how he had given the hearing of one of his ears to the boy and how the fisherman's wife had warm-held his face.

Bright Blue's barely-there eyes filled with tears as he said, 'That was the first time I have ever been warm-held. The glow in me is so big that I cannot contain it. My all-on-my-ownness has gone.'

Malock wise-eyed the merrow and said, 'What you are

feeling is the summer-meadow sweetness of The Beautiful Belong.'

The News of the Hill

By the time the bluebells were in the woods, The Beautiful Belong in Bright Blue was so big that the ghosts of The Big Deep no longer haunted him in his sleep.

Bright Blue spent his days sitting on the rocks, repairing the nets of the fishermen. Late in the day, when the boats came in, he helped the fishermen to land their catches, and they were mighty thankful for his strong arms. Most none of the fishermen felt sick anymore when they saw Bright Blue, but most all of them had tears in their eyes when they saw the hot hurt burning into him as the healing of the holy clay wore off.

Every day, the wives of the fishermen took it in turns to pack fat baskets of food for Bright Blue. They took the baskets down to the rocks and good-companied him. They told him the fast and slow news of the hill, and they all warm-held his face when they took leave of him.

Every evening, when the sun sank into the sea, Bright Blue returned to his cave, slop-slathered the clay on to the bits of him that hurt the most and waited for the moon to rise and for Malock to sit up from the ground. Malock was always pleased to see Bright Blue. The bones of the holy man fleshed up with the food that Bright Blue shared with him, and the ears of the holy man twitched as he listened to the fast and slow news of the hill.

As the sea breeze warmed and the days stretched out their big blue skies, it was Bright Blue's kindness that became the fast news of the hill.

⊱⋅⊷⊷⊙⊶⊷⋅⊰

On the Very Long Day, when the sun had climbed to the roof of the sky, the fisherman's wife who had first warm-held the merrow came down to the rocks with her basket. She did not wear her usual smile, and her eyes were all teary'd up.

'Bright Blue, today my news is sad. I do not want to heavy your heart with the telling of it.' As she spoke, she shook her head slowly and lowered her eyes to the ground.

Bright Blue gentled her and said, 'Please empty your words into my ear if it will lighten your own heart to do so.'

And so the fisherman's wife poured the news into the merrow's ear.

'The young farmer at the back of the hill has taken a fever that is boiling his lungs and bloodying his cough. The doctor says that it's time to call the priest. I cannot see how his wife and four children will survive without him.'

When Bright Blue heard the words of the fisherman's wife, the hurt of them went straight to his eyes and the heavy of them went straight to his heart. He asked the fisherman's wife to take him to the farmer at the back of the hill right away.

The farmer was just about to go to the Above-the-Sky place when Bright Blue got to his bedside. The merrow could not bear the sorry of it all, so he cut out one of his own lungs, divided it in two and put the pair of healthy bellows into the farmer's chest. The farmer breathed deep and easy and his fever cooled.

Bright Blue turned to the farmer's wife and said, 'I have lungs the size of a whale's and plenty of breath to spare. Your husband will not need the priest today.'

The farmer's wife warm-held Bright Blue's face, and Bright Blue's heart glowed big inside him. The farmer's wife gave Bright Blue a pot of her husband's best poteen, and her four children waved the merrow back down to the shore.

That evening, Bright Blue returned to his cave and waited for the moon to rise. When the night sky was all lit, Malock sat up from the ground. As Bright Blue slop-slathered the clay on to the bits of him that hurt the most, he shared the poteen with the holy man and told him about the farmer and his wife and their four children. Malock's ears twitched as the merrow told him how he had given the farmer one of his lungs.

When Bright Blue had finished, Malock wise-eyed the merrow, nodded and said, 'This is good news.'

On the day the briar berries ripened, a fisherman's wife with the cool of winter in her greying hair came down to the rocks with her basket. She wore no smile, and her eyes were all teary'd up.

'Bright Blue, today my news is sad. I do not want to heavy your heart with the telling of it.' As she spoke, she shook her head slowly and lowered her eyes to the ground.

Bright Blue gentled her and said, 'Please empty your words into my ear if it will lighten your own heart to do so.'

And so the fisherman's wife poured the news into the merrow's ear.

'The old woman who lives at the side of the hill is dying from a broken heart. Her husband and three sons were taken by the sea the night you arrived at Murlough Bay, and she is worsening by the day. The folk who live at the side of the hill say that she talks of throwing herself into the sea from the cliffs at Fair Head.'

When Bright Blue heard the words of the fisherman's wife, the hurt of them went straight to his eyes and the heavy of them went straight to his heart. He asked the fisherman's wife to take him to the old woman at the side of the hill right away.

When Bright Blue and the fisherman's wife got to the old woman's cottage, they found her alone, rocking to-and-fro on her chair. No fire was burning, the cupboards were bare and grief had stolen the old woman's tongue and tears.

The merrow could not bear the sorry of it all, so he cut out a piece of his own heart and put it in the chest of the old woman. The old woman's eyes flooded with thank yous and the edges of her mouth bent into the beginning of a smile.

'Old woman, the heart I give to you is big enough, soft enough and brave enough to cradle you through your grief. It will bring you great comfort to know that the souls of your husband and three sons went straight to the Above-the-Sky place. I saw them go there with my own eyes.'

The old woman warm-held Bright Blue's face, and Bright Blue's heart glowed big inside him. She gave him a soft blanket to cosy himself with at night, and then she waved him back to the shore.

>·+◊·–○·◊+·◁

That evening, Bright Blue returned to his cave and waited for the moon to rise. When the night sky was all lit, Malock sat up from the ground. As Bright Blue slop-slathered the clay on to the bits of him that hurt the most, he warmed the bones of the holy man in the blanket and told him about the old woman. Malock's ears twitched as the merrow told him how he had given the old woman a piece of his heart.

When Bright Blue had finished, Malock wise-eyed the merrow, nodded and said, 'This is good news.'

But sometimes it turns out that what is good news for one person is bad news for another. And, as the sea breeze cooled to a bite and the days shortened to a blink, it was Bright Blue's best news that would eventually turn into the worst news of all.

The Best News

On The Very Short Day, when the sun had used up all of its shine and barely bothered to rise, a fisherman's wife with crinkles of kindness around her peat-dark eyes came down to the rocks with her basket.

The fisherman's wife was not on her own – in one hand she held the fat basket of food for Bright Blue, and in the other she held the hand of a cloaked young woman.

The fisherman's wife did not come straight to the rocks where Bright Blue was sitting. Instead, she walked with the young woman down to the beach, took a blanket from the basket and laid it on to the sand. She took the young woman's hand and guided her on to the blanket. The young woman sat down, pulled her billowing cloak tight around her and turned her face to the wind.

The fisherman's wife then made her way over to Bright Blue. She sat next to Bright Blue and good-companied him and told him the fast and slow news of the hill. But she did not mention the young woman in the cloak once.

The itch of curiosity grew too big for Bright Blue. He nodded over to the young woman, and said to the fisherman's wife, 'Tell me the story of the girl in the cloak.'

The smile of the fisherman's wife faded, and her eyes teary'd up.

'Bright Blue, the story is so sad that most everyone who hears it doesn't have enough tears for it. I do not want to heavy your heart with the telling of it.' As she spoke, she shook her head slowly and lowered her eyes to the ground.

Bright Blue gentled her and said, 'Please empty her story into my ear if it will lighten your own heart to do so.'

And so the fisherman's wife poured the story into the merrow's ear.

'That is Daughter McCormick and she lives in The Big House at the top of the hill. When she was cut out of Wife McCormick's belly, the priest asked us all to say Big Sunday Prayers: when God made Daughter McCormick, He forgot to give her eyes.

'Daughter McCormick will be twenty when the next snow falls, and no one has ever heard her complain about her misfortune. A seam of gentleness runs right through her bones, and she is as hopeful and bright as the spring. But Wife McCormick took it stone hard, and the whole thing soured her up. Husband McCormick left the hill because he got lost in the hurt of it. Wife McCormick has never warm-held her daughter and only lets her out of The Big House once a year – on The Very Short Day.

'The whole hill feels heart-sore sorry for Daughter McCormick, so on the day she is allowed out we take it in turns to bring her to her favourite place – the beach below Benvan. Today is her outside day, and today it is my turn.'

As Bright Blue heard the words of the fisherman's wife, the hurt of them went straight to his eyes, and the heavy of them went straight to his heart. 'If today is her outside day, then we should be good-companying her,' said Bright Blue. 'Her all-on-my-ownness must be as big as the sky.'

<hr>

When the fisherman's wife and Bright Blue reached the place where Daughter McCormick was sitting, she pulled down the hood of her cloak, turned her face towards them and warm-welcomed them.

Bright Blue's almost-there eyes burned at the sight of her. She was prettier than any merrowmaid he'd ever seen, and her voice soothed the burn of his wounds even faster than Malock's clay. The golden waves of her hair billowed all about her in the wind, and he could see her filling her heart up with the song of the sea.

'Won't you tell me what the sea looks like today?' Daughter McCormick asked.

The fisherman's wife nodded at Bright Blue, a big smile crinkling her face.

'Daughter McCormick, today the sea looks so savage-beautiful that I cannot describe it. You'd have to see it with your own eyes,' Bright Blue told her.

Daughter McCormick felt the sharp of his words and would have cried tears the size of puddles if she could have. But Bright Blue had no intention of hurting her. He heaved himself up on to his hobbling legs and made his way to the water's edge. Then he pulled out his best eye and divided it in two. He dipped the two red eyes into the salty water, and when he lifted them out, not only had they turned a beautiful sea-green, but they had also grown to the perfect size and were full of the mystery of the ocean.

He returned to Daughter McCormick and gentled her, 'Daughter McCormick, though my eyes are small, they can deep-see like an octopus. I have plenty of seeing to spare, and I am happy to share my eyes with you. Today you will see the sea with your own eyes, and you will also see me. The sea is so savage-beautiful that it will help you to cry your first tears, but I am so savage-ugly that I will make your new eyes hurt.'

Bright Blue took the two green eyes and rolled them into the right place on Daughter McCormick's face.

Daughter McCormick turned her face to the sea and wide-eyed it all in and cried her first tears. Then she turned her face to Bright Blue and wide-eyed him all in, but her new eyes didn't hurt at all. She looked directly into Bright Blue's remaining eye and said, 'The glow in me is so big that I cannot contain it. My all-on-my-ownness was as big as the sky, but now it is gone.'

Daughter McCormick warm-held Bright Blue's face and true-told him that he was savage-beautiful. Bright Blue's heart glowed so big inside him that he shone like the summer sun.

Bright Blue watched Daughter McCormick and the fisherman's wife wind their way up the hillside, into the mist. When they had disappeared, he picked up his basket and hobbled to the cave. He could not wait for the moon to rise so that he could share his news with Malock.

⊷⊶⊷⊶○⊶⊷⊶⊷

When the night sky was all lit, Malock sat up from the ground. As the holy man helped himself to the contents of the basket, Bright Blue told him the high and the low of it, the wide and the narrow of it and the inside-out of it. And all the while that Bright Blue spoke, he shone like the summer sun.

When Bright Blue had finished, Malock wise-eyed the merrow, nodded and said, 'This is the best news. The big glow inside you is not the summer-meadow sweetness of The Beautiful Belong. What you are feeling is the deep-root comfort of The Beautiful Belong-Together.'

As Bright Blue slop-slathered the clay on to the bits of him that hurt the most, Malock told him all about The Beautiful Belong-Together. He told the merrow how it could break your heart and mend your heart, and how it could small you right down and big you right up. He told the merrow about how you could keep The Beautiful Belong-Together and how you could lose it. He told the merrow how you could holy yourself to someone so you could stay with them even when you went to the Above-the-Sky place.

Bright Blue was now shining so brightly that the whole cave was lit up like a church at Candlemas. 'Thank you for the wise of your words, holy man. I will look after The Beautiful Belong-Together as best I can. You are right – this is the best news.'

'The best news? The best news?' cawed a high-pitched voice from the shadows close to Malock's bed. 'You're wrong. This is the worst news.'

When the cawing stopped, a crow of a woman moved close enough to the cave for Bright Blue's glow to reveal the full ugly of her. Her lips curled like big winter waves. Her eyes hot-sparked like a blacksmith's forge. Her thin white hair strained to free itself from the regiment of pins that were pushed into her head. Her skin was so tight you could see the bone of her through it. Her crooked nose pecked at the wind, and she was full of empty.

She set the burn of her eyes on Bright Blue and Hell-furied at him. 'I am Wife McCormick. You have bad-magicked my daughter, and now she is full of The Beautiful Belong-Together. But let me tell you that no daughter of mine will holy herself to a monster like you. Now that she has eyes, I will have no trouble getting a gentleman from Ballycastle to take her for a wife. A rich gentleman, might I add, who will pay me for the privilege. I am ordering you to be gone from this place before the sun rises!'

Her rage was so hot that her black skirts started to steam in the winter air. Malock was so frightened of her that he lay back down. But Bright Blue was not frightened of her at all. The merrow knew he was safe on sacred ground, and The Beautiful Belong-Together had bigged him right up.

'I will not go, Wife McCormick. I do not mean to make you angry, but this is my home and I am going to stay here. If your daughter wishes to holy herself to me, then so be it.' Bright Blue brave-eyed Wife McCormick for a little longer than he should have.

She spat him straight in the eye and sharp-pointed her finger at him like a knife. 'If you do not go, I will make you.'

Wife McCormick lifted her skirts, turned on her heel and flapped back into the night.

The Witches of Barnish

The very next morning, Wife McCormick set about putting a worry worm into the heads of the people on the hill. She told the fishermen halfway up the hill that Bright Blue would poison the fish in the bay. She told the people at the back of the hill that Bright Blue would steal their children. She told the people at the side of the hill that Bright Blue would eat up their souls and leave them full of empty. She told the people on the top of the hill that Bright Blue was a demon.

But no one let the worry worm in. Everyone soft-butter-heart-loved the merrow.

Wife McCormick was as determined as driving snow and as wily as a fox. She decided that if she could not make the people of the hill chase Bright Blue away, then she would have him bad-magicked away by the witches of Barnish.

⋗⋯⬥⋯⊙⋯⬦⋯⋖

As the sun slid down the sky, Wife McCormick hard-galloped down the back of the hill to Barnish.

She knocked on the door of the witches' house then pushed her way bold-as-you-like right in. The three witches jumped back from the cauldron they were stirring and dropped their big wooden spoons. They put on their poor-little-old-lady faces as quickly as they could and started humbling themselves before Wife McCormick.

'We're not stirring up any trouble, lady. We're just three old girls cooking up a hot supper, trying to keep warm,' said the first witch, magicking up a set of sad-puppy eyes and shrinking herself all small.

'Will you sit by the fire with me and let me read some of The Good Book to you, lady?' piped up the second witch, who had magicked herself into a rocking chair by the hearth.

'Will you pray with me for those who will be cold and hungry this winter, lady?' implored the third witch, who had magicked herself a right holy face and was kneeling on the floor with her gnarly hands clasped in prayer.

'Pardon me. I must have been mistaken,' clevered Wife McCormick. 'I wish you a pleasant evening.' Wife McCormick made to leave, but then turned back and said, 'Oh, if you should happen to see the three witches of Barnish, will you tell them that I am prepared to give a mighty fine reward in exchange for some of their bad-magick? I've heard that their bad-magick is the best bad-magick in these parts.'

Well, the first witch was bursting with pride and couldn't help but grow herself big again and say, 'Oh yes, it is the best bad-magick in these parts, lady.'

Wife McCormick pretended not to notice that the first witch had grown herself big again and continued, 'And will you tell them that the reward will be the heart of a merrow?'

Well, the second witch was bursting with the grab-it and couldn't help but drop The Good Book on the floor and show her true self to Wife McCormick. 'Oh yes, them witches would be interested in one of them merrow hearts, lady. They could do some devilish good bad-magick with a heart like that.'

Wife McCormick pretended not to notice that the second witch had dropped her disguise, and continued, 'And will you let them know that, if I cannot find them, I'll have to take the offer to the witches in—'

Before Wife McCormick had finished speaking, the third witch had magicked herself between Wife McCormick and the door, and there was not a shadow of the holy about her any more.

'Them witches are no good. No good at all. Don't you take that offer to them,' warned the third witch, as she showed herself fully to Wife McCormick.

'Well, where can I find the three witches of Barnish then?' asked Wife McCormick, all little-girl innocent. 'I would much prefer to give my business to them.'

'We can get a message to the Barnish witches, lady. Just tell us what you need from them in exchange for the heart of the merrow,' the third witch assured her, all holy again.

Wife McCormick told them that she wanted the merrow away from Murlough Bay. She told them that she never wanted him to come back and that she wanted the witches to bad-magick him until his heart stopped beating.

The three witches nodded slowly as she spoke, taking the big black of it right in. When Wife McCormick had finished, the first witch got up and said, 'I will take the message to them right away. Wait here.'

The first witch stepped out of the front door and closed it behind her. In less than a blink of an eye, she stepped back in and said, 'The witches have listened to your request, but they are in last-chance big trouble at the moment. If they bad-magick the merrow until his heart stops beating, the likely of it is that all three of them will have their necks stretched. But they are mighty interested in that merrow heart and have found a way to help you.'

The first witch explained that in order to stop the heart of a merrow beating, you have to dry every drop of the sea out of him. She lowered her voice, leaned smell-your-breath close to Wife McCormick and whispered, 'To dry every drop of the sea out of him, you have to burn him.'

The second witch lowered her voice, leaned smell-your-breath close to Wife McCormick and whispered, 'Them witches are going to show you how to catch the merrow and how to dry him out.'

The third witch lowered her voice, leaned smell-your-breath close to Wife McCormick and whispered, 'Them witches are going to give you four of their best bad-magick potions.'

All three witches stayed close to Wife McCormick and

magick-eyed her, raising their eyebrows and nodding their heads expectantly.

'It is a very good offer, and it's a rare thing for them witches to make an offer as good as that,' said the first witch. 'Will you take it while they still like you, lady?'

Wife McCormick slow-nodded her head, and the three witches taught her all through the night. When the grey of the morning came, Wife McCormick knew how to catch the merrow, how to dry him out and how to make his heart stop beating.

The Merrow Cage

Wife McCormick pulled up the hood of her cloak and slipped out of the witches' house into the thick morning mist.

It was almost a year to the day since Bright Blue had been tail-slapped on to the beach at Murlough Bay, and Wife McCormick was determined to make this day the merrow's last. She had gulped down the witches' lessons like a top-of-the-class student and was going to do exactly as they had said.

On her way back from Barnish, Wife McCormick stopped by a swathe of bare willows that bent and swayed in the biting wind. She cut a single branch and took it with her. Then she hard-galloped it back to The Big House at the top of the hill and waited until dusk smeared itself across the sky.

When it was dark enough for her to hide in the shadows, Wife McCormick took the branch of willow, a bag containing the bad-magick potions and a hessian sack, and hard-galloped it across the top of the hill to Lough Doo.

She planted the willow branch in the soft ground next to the lough. She opened her bag and took out the first bad-magick potion. Just as the witches had taught her, she poured the potion on to the branch and stood well back.

The ground around the willow heaved, spluttered and squelched as the branch fast-grew itself into a willow cage.

Next, Wife McCormick took her hessian sack and went listening for a sheep with a very noisy, break-your-heart bleat. As soon as she heard the bleat, she took her hessian sack and pushed the sheep inside it. She dragged the sack into the willow cage, opened her bag and took out the second bad-magick potion. Just as the witches had taught her, she opened the sack, poured the potion into the mouth of the sheep, closed the sack and stood well back.

The sack rumpled its way around the inside of the cage as the bleating of the sheep turned into the crying of a human baby.

Next, Wife McCormick hid in the rushes by Lough Doo and waited, just as the witches had taught her.

⊱────⊰

At the bottom of the hill, Bright Blue and Malock were yarning to each other as usual. Malock was unpacking the fat basket of food as Bright Blue slop-slathered the clay on to the bits of him that hurt the most. Malock had just started telling the story of a man who was sainted up by mistake when Bright Blue suddenly stopped listening to him.

'Are you tired of my stories, merrow?' sighed Malock.

'Do you hear that?' asked Bright Blue as he leaned out of the cave and turned his hearing ear towards Lough Doo.

'I hear only the wind and the sea,' answered the holy man.

'I hear a baby crying, Malock, and it is such a terrible, lonely sound. That cry is full of all-on-my-ownness, and it's more than my ear can bear. I'm going to see if the child needs help,' said Bright Blue.

Malock watched as Bright Blue hobbled into the night, following the sound of the baby's cries.

⊱────⊰

When he got to Lough Doo, Bright Blue saw the cage and the sack inside it. He horrored at the grim of it and sorried for the soul of the man or woman who had left the poor child out on the hill.

He opened the door of the cage and leaned in to pull out the pitiful bundle. Just as his hands touched the sack, Wife McCormick leapt out of the shadows and whack-walloped the back of Bright Blue's head with a stone, just as the witches had taught her.

As Bright Blue lay senseless-still at the cage's entrance, Wife McCormick worked as quickly as she could. She hauled him into the cage, opened her bag and took out the third bad-magick potion. She opened Bright Blue's mouth, poured the potion into him and stood well back, just as the witches had taught her.

Bright Blue's body writhed and fitted. A sulphur-yellow foam leaked out of his mouth. Eventually his body lay as still as a corpse on a slab.

Wife McCormick crawled into the willow cage. She tethered the wrists of the merrow to the bars of the cage. She rusty-nailed his barnacled legs to the base of the cage and unhooked his rotting feet so that he could not run away when the bad-magick potion wore off.

She opened her bag, took out the last bad-magick potion and emptied the contents of the bottle all over the merrow, all over the sheep in the sack and all over the willow cage. Then Wife McCormick crawled out of the cage and locked the door behind her.

Next, Wife McCormick put her mouth to the bars of the cage, blew as hard as she could and stood well back, just as the witches had taught her.

The white-hot fingers of long-dead men pushed up out of the boggy ground. The fingers wrapped themselves around the bars of the cage, then reached inside and wrapped themselves around Bright Blue and around the sack. As the fingers tightened their hold, the knuckles sparked blue and the fingers burst into flame.

Wife McCormick smiled as she watched the flames eat up the cage.

But she should not have smiled.

She should not have smiled because she had not put *all* of the merrow into the cage.

The Worst News of All

In the fisherman's cottage halfway up the hill, the little boy with the merrow's hearing sat up in his bed and called out to his parents.

'Can you hear that?' asked the little boy.

'I hear only the wind and the sea,' said the fisherman.

'I hear a baby crying, and it is such a terrible, lonely sound.

The cry is full of all-on-my-ownness, and it's making my ears hurt. We should find the child and bring it to safety,' wept the little boy.

The fisherman, his wife and the little boy set out into the night to find the baby. The little boy followed the lonely sound, and, as they made their way up towards Lough Doo, they called on the other fishermen and asked them to help with the search.

At the back of the hill, the farmer with the merrow's lungs spluttered himself awake and started to cough and wheeze like a dirty chimney.

'Wife, our house is on fire!' cried the farmer.

'Our house is not on fire, husband,' gentled the farmer's wife as she breathed in the cold, clean winter air that filled their farmhouse.

'Well, my lungs can feel a fire, and it's close to us. I'm going to rouse the other farmers from the back of the hill, and we'll find it and put it out,' wheezed the farmer as he pulled on his boots.

The farmer hurried into the winter night, taking a beater for the flames with him.

In no time at all, a band of farmers armed with beaters were following the farmer with the merrow's lungs up towards Lough Doo.

At the side of the hill, the old woman with the merrow's heart woke up with a dark ache in her chest. Her heart was full of heavy, and it spoke straight to her head.

'Something bad is happening out on the hill tonight,' it whispered.

The old woman wrapped herself in her cloak and scuttled to every neighbour at the side of the hill. She banged on every door until it was opened and said, 'There is something bad happening out on the hill tonight. Can you feel it?'

Not one of them could feel it, but when they saw the fear in the old woman's eyes, the men from the side of the hill closed their doors behind them and followed her up towards Lough Doo.

On the top of the hill, Daughter McCormick was looking out of her window and enjoying her merrow eyes when she saw angry flames leaping to the top of the sky.

She rushed into Wife McCormick's room to waken her, but her bed was empty. Daughter McCormick ran as fast as she could to the closest neighbours to alert them.

When she got to the first door, she banged on it until it was opened. She pointed up towards Lough Doo and cried, 'We must wake up the top of the hill: there's a fire coming! The flames are so hot that they are burning a hole in the sky.'

But her neighbour looked out into the night and said, 'I can't see any flames. I see only the stars and the moon.'

Out of the darkness, a voice shouted, 'She's right! There's a demon fire raging somewhere up there, and we're going to find it and beat it out. Will you bring the men from the top of the hill to help us?'

The farmer from the back of the hill walked out of the shadows, and an army of twenty men stood behind him.

Daughter McCormick's neighbour pulled on his coat and went to wake up the top of the hill. Then the men from the top of the hill took their beaters and joined the men from the back of the hill.

'I can see exactly where the fire is. I will take you to it,' said Daughter McCormick.

The men thanked her for her help, and together they all bent into the wind and pushed their way up towards Lough Doo.

>-•→>-○-<←•-<

As Wife McCormick smugged and smiled at the burning cage in front of her, she did not notice the fishermen and the little boy from halfway up the hill approaching her from behind.

As Wife McCormick rubbed her hands together and crowed into the wind, she did not notice the old woman and the men from the side of the hill approaching her from her right.

As Wife McCormick raised her skirts and danced in the

cindered mud, she did not notice Daughter McCormick and the men from the back and the top of the hill approaching her from her left.

The little boy with the merrow's hearing ran up to Wife McCormick and tugged at her skirts to get her attention.

'What are you doing? Can't you hear the baby crying? Why are you letting the baby burn?' The little boy made his voice loud enough for the whole of the hill to hear him.

When the men from the back of the hill and the top of the hill heard that there was a baby in the flames, they all rushed forwards with their beaters. They showed no fear as they plunged themselves into the heat, their eyes clouded with tears as they felt the full sad of it.

But for all their beating, the flames grew bigger.

Wife McCormick couldn't contain herself any longer. All full of wicked, she hopped up and down on the spot and squawked, 'You'll never put out those flames because they are bad-magick flames. You'd need a thousand beaters to put that fire out. And you'll never rescue that child because there is no child. When those flames finish their job, all that will be left is a well-cooked sheep with the break-your-heart bleat burned out of it.'

The men lowered their beaters.

All eyes were on Wife McCormick.

'Oh, yes – how silly of me! I nearly forgot,' sniggered Wife McCormick. 'A dried-out merrow will also be left.'

'We will not let you burn Bright Blue!' roared the farmer from the back of the hill.

The whole of the hill watched as the farmer took big-boot strides to the edge of the flames. He stretched his arms wide, dropped his head right back, filled up his powerful merrow lungs with the whirling wind and blew as hard as he could. A blast of winter as strong as ten thousand fire-beaters howled out of him and put the fire out.

A curtain of smoke pulled itself back to reveal the full grim of the cage.

Only the rusty nails remained of Bright Blue's barnacled timber legs. His rotting feet smoked in a corner. The tar of his waist joint was burning him to his bones. The skin on his face ran like wax. His remaining eye was wide-stare open and full of fear. He was crying tears of the worst kind of hurt. His all-on-my-ownness was so big that you could have seen it from the moon. The beat of his heart was so slow that it had almost come to a stop.

As the whole of the hill ran to the cage to help Bright Blue, no one noticed Wife McCormick slip away into the night shadows.

The fishermen from halfway up the hill carefully carried Bright Blue down to Malock's ruined church by the sea. The men from the back of the hill, the side of the hill and the top of the hill walked silently behind them, and the little boy, the farmer, the old woman and Daughter McCormick walked silently in front.

When they got to Malock's church, the holy man sat up from the ground and told them to dig a bed in the clay next to his own bed. He told them to lay the body of Bright Blue into the hole. He told them to cover the merrow with the clay, leaving only his face clear.

When this was done, Daughter McCormick warm-held Bright Blue's face and lullabied him. Her song filled the cold sky with the warm glow of The Beautiful Belong-Together, and the stars stood still as they listened.

The old woman from the side of the hill took the worst kind of hurt out of Bright Blue's heart and put it into her own. She cradled and cosied the hurt until it didn't hurt any more.

The farmer from the back of the hill filled up his lungs, leaned over the merrow's face and summer-breezed the fear out of Bright Blue's eye.

The little boy from halfway up the hill listened for the loudest words inside the heads of the people of the whole of the hill and spoke them into Bright Blue's ear.

'Thank you,' said the little boy.

Malock holied Daughter McCormick to Bright Blue as fast as he could, and then the whole of the hill stood around Bright Blue's bed as Malock covered the merrow's face with clay.

Malock looked up and said, 'Let him sleep.'

The End(s)

Most people say that Bright Blue went into The Big Long Dream that night.

But there are some people who say that Slap came up from The Big Deep that night. They say that he awful-sorried to Bright Blue and the walking men, that he told them that he had realised that most all walking men were good men and promised that the merrowmen would never trap the soul of a good walking man again. They say that Slap gave Bright Blue back his bluer-than-a-mackerel tail and took him back to The Big Deep.

And there are others who say that the holy clay miracled the merrow full well again. They say that the whole of the hill worked together to make him new legs that didn't hurt him, and that he lived out his days with Daughter McCormick and their many children, grandchildren and great-grandchildren.

I'm sorry to say that I can't tell you the full true of what happened that winter night. The full true of it is that no one really knows what happened, because the walking men who were up at Lough Doo that night had heads wise enough to mystery the true of it right up.

But I can tell you that if you ever go to Murlough Bay, you will most likely notice that the people in these parts are no ordinary walking men. The people in these parts have eyes that can see right into you, ears that can hear your thoughts, lungs that can blow the leaves off the trees and hearts that are big enough, soft enough and brave enough to cosy the hurt right out of you.

⊷─◈─○─◈─⊶

Oh, and I nearly forgot to warn you that you should be wide-awake careful if you ever find yourself on the road between Barnish and the back of the hill. I've heard tell of three little old ladies who wander that road most every night looking for Wife McCormick and the merrow's heart that she owes them.

And as for Wife McCormick ... most everyone says that she left for America on one of those big ships. They say that, on the way to America, the light went out in the sky and the water scary-swirled up. They say that something chewed the hull right out of the bottom of the ship and that, just before it went down, there was an almighty, ear-splitting ... SLAP.

The SONG of HULVA

Verse 1

One night, so long ago that only the storytellers remember it, a star died and fell out of the sky. It was only a young star, but it had sparkled too brightly and used up all of its shine.

When the star's mother saw that her child was dead, she didn't want to hang in the sky any more. She cried all of her remaining shine on to the child, and then she died and fell to the ground too.

The mother and child lay together on the ground, and the earth covered them up and soft-blanket-comforted them. And after a while, from the ground where the stars lay, there grew a holly tree.

The holly tree was called Hulva, and Hulva greened the ground with enough children to grow a wood all around her. The wood was called Breen Wood, and Hulva became its queen. She loved her children well enough for their roots to grow deep and strong, and despite the hurt of long, dark winters, all of her children thrived.

The wind sang the Song of Hulva to faraway trees in dying places. The faraway trees asked the wind to carry their children to Hulva for safekeeping. The wind lifted their children and took them to Hulva, and she loved them into the ground. Their roots grew deep and strong, and despite the hurt of long, dark winters, all of her new children thrived.

As the years passed, the wood grew larger and denser. At the heart of it, sharp holly swayed amongst curvy-leafed oak. Around the edges of it, young downy birch beckoned the birds, the deer and the wolves. Hazel made holy places and faerie wells, and alder stood watch over cool ponds and clear streams.

As the years passed, Hulva grew old-beautiful and gentle-wise. Her evergreen leaves held the hope of summer in them all year round. When the wood took its winter sleep, Hulva and the younger holly remained awake and lullabied the other children.

As a mother, she taught her children how to love. As a queen, she taught her children how to grow together.

⊢┄⊷⊶○⊷⊶┄⊣

When the sun was too tired to shine and the snow was deep enough to drown in, the wind visited Hulva. The wind carried the smell of burning peat into the clearing at the heart of the wood and curled it all around the queen.

'What is this news, wind?' asked Hulva.

'This is the news of a village called Crann, Hulva. As you have grown your wood, the people of Crann have grown their

122

village. It lies not five fields from here. Today, a son of Crann will visit you.'

The wind held its breath so Hulva could hear the slow, rhythmic thud of footsteps breaking into the wood.

Hulva told the holly to stop lullabying and stay swayless-still. The chiming icicles that hung from the branches froze themselves silent. The deer and the wolves shadowed into white ghosts.

Hulva watched as a young, rabbit-eyed man with a knapsack on his back and an axe in one hand waded into the clearing at the heart of the wood. He turned full-circle and let his gaze crawl over each tree.

After a while he shook his head, shrugged his shoulders and made ready to leave. But at that very moment, one of the oaks turned over in his sleep. The man nodded at the restless oak, swung his axe back and brought it down hard, the blade cleaving deep into the oak's trunk. Then he pulled out the axe and struck the oak again and again until he fell over, severed from his roots.

Hulva's branches blistered with blood and her roots curled up at the cruel of it. The holly started to cry for their brother but, fearful that the axe would cut into them too, Hulva shushed and stilled them.

The man dropped his axe, took the knapsack off his back and pulled an ox horn from it. He blew into the horn three times, and the wind carried the news to Crann.

In no time at all, three men with faces full of autumn but limbs full of spring, waded into the snowy clearing. They tied the oak up with a thick rope and dragged him away.

Hulva sang moonfuls of mourning songs until the bloody blisters on her branches healed. She planted the memory of her stolen son in the ground so that the wood could grow tender-tough from it. And, when the rest of her children woke from their winter sleep, she gentled them and couraged them and loved them more than before.

➤┈◆┈○┈◆┈◄

When the sun was too hot to bear the company of clouds and the sky was big enough to dream in, the wind visited Hulva. The wind carried the smell of smoke and sawdust into the clearing at the heart of the wood and curled it all around the queen.

'What is this news, wind?' asked Hulva.

'This is the news of your restless son, Hulva. The wood-cutter took a knife to him and bladed the skin from his flesh. The woodcutter burned your son's skin and enjoyed the warmth and the comforting smell of it. Then he chopped his flesh and chiselled it and turned it and smoothed it and grooved it. The woodcutter made your son into a cradle which now holds his new daughter.'

Hulva's bark wrinkled and her leaves sharpened at the savage of it.

The wind wound itself around Hulva's trunk and squeezed her until she gasped for breath.

'The villagers like the cradle, Hulva. They want more of your children. They will send the woodcutter to you every winter from now on.'

Verse 2

The first winter the woodcutter returned, he took the smallest birch in the wood. She was not the youngest of Hulva's children, but she was the weakest. Her roots were too feeble to feed from the earth, so she hardly grew at all.

Hulva's branches blistered with blood and her roots curled up at the cruel of it.

Hulva sang moonfuls of mourning songs until the bloody blisters on her branches healed. She planted the memory of her daughter in the ground so that the wood could grow tender-tough from it. And, when her other children woke from their winter sleep, she gentled them and couraged them and loved them more than before.

When the sun was too bright to look at and the grass was sweet enough to grow fat on, the wind visited Hulva. The wind carried the smell of wholesome broth into the clearing at the heart of the wood and curled it all around the queen.

'What is this news, wind?' asked Hulva.

'This is the news of your hungriest daughter, Hulva. The woodcutter has made her into a bowl for the blacksmith.'

Hulva's bark wrinkled and her leaves sharpened at the savage of it.

⊷•○•⊶

The second winter the woodcutter returned, he took the biggest oak in the wood. He was not only the strongest of Hulva's children, but also the wisest.

Hulva's branches blistered with blood and her roots curled up at the cruel of it.

Hulva sang moonfuls of mourning songs until the bloody blisters on her branches healed. She planted the memory of her son in the ground so the wood could grow tender-tough from it. And, when her other children woke up from their winter sleep, she gentled them and couraged them and loved them more than before.

When the sun was too high for the birds to reach and the barleycorn was golden enough to grow rich on, the wind visited Hulva. The wind carried the sound of a church bell into the clearing at the heart of the wood and rang it all around the queen.

'What is this news, wind?' asked Hulva.

'This is the news of your strongest and wisest son, Hulva. The woodcutter has made him into a church pew.'

Hulva's bark wrinkled and her leaves sharpened at the savage of it.

━┽◆━○━◆┾━

The third winter the woodcutter returned, he took the oldest hazel in the wood. He was not only the kindest of Hulva's children, but also the loneliest, and he often ached for company.

Hulva's branches blistered with blood and her roots curled up at the cruel of it.

But this time, Hulva did not sing moonfuls of mourning songs. The bloody blisters on her branches did not heal. She planted the memory of her son in the ground, but she did not want the wood to grow tender from it, only tough. And, when her remaining children woke up from their winter sleep, she did not gentle them. Instead, she promised that she would keep them safe and that no more children would be taken.

When the sun was too heavy to hang so high and the harvest was good enough to winter on, the wind visited Hulva. The wind carried the sound of an old man coughing into the clearing at the heart of the wood and spluttered it all around the queen.

'What is this news, wind?' asked Hulva.

'This is the news of your kindest and loneliest son, Hulva.

The woodcutter has made him into a walking stick for a crooked old man.'

Hulva's bark did not wrinkle. But her leaves steel-sharpened and cut the wind and made it bleed.

The wind whipped up into the sky for safety, but Hulva lashed her scissor-branches upwards and wound them around the wind's throat.

'I do not like the woodcutter, wind,' said Hulva. 'Bring him to me at the deepest dark.'

Verse 3

The wind returned to the village of Crann and blasted the villagers into their homes. For three moons, it barked and blew and scoffed and slew. It scoured the fields bare, stole away the cattle's winter feed and tore the dead out of their graves. It haunted down chimneys, pushed against doors, and ghosted the warmth from every stone floor.

Then, at the deepest dark, when the sun was too weak to wake up and the frost was sharp enough to bite the soul out of a body, the wind stilled itself.

The woodcutter sent up big thank you prayers. His family was hollow with hunger because he had not yet felled a winter tree and so he had no furniture to sell. Now that the wind had stopped, he could finally go to the wood.

He swaddled himself in furs, slung his knapsack across his back and fetched his axe. He kissed the cheeks of his new son, who was sleeping in his oak cradle. He stroked the head of his three-summers-old daughter. He nodded to his old, paper-skinned mother. He gentled his young wife with his mittened hands and tendered her with his eyes.

'I will go into the wood now and fetch a good tree. The shepherd wants a chair for his mother to rock in. He will pay me as soon as I have the wood to make it, and we will have food for the rest of winter.' The woodcutter opened the door of his tiny cottage and looked out into the slow-falling snow. 'I will be back for supper.'

⊳⊷⊙⊶⊲

As the woodcutter made his way into the wood, the snow stopped falling. Only his boots and his beating heart were moving. Everything else was silent and slow-freezing still.

When the woodcutter reached the heart of the wood, he turned full-circle and let his gaze crawl over each tree.

Hulva prickled her leaves to get his attention, and the woodcutter nodded at her. He fixed his eyes on her silver bark and drove the axe towards her, but Hulva lifted her roots from the ground and moved out of its path. The woodcutter lost his balance and fell forwards into the snow.

Hulva told the younger holly to close their eyes and start lullabying the sleeping wood. Their voices were feather-soft and full of home. Hulva joined in, and her voice was full of cradle-comfort and motherly-tender. The lullaby drowsied the woodcutter and warmed him all the way through. He dropped his axe and tugged off his knapsack. Then he took off his furs, his boots and his clothes and lay down in the snow.

Hulva's voice pulled him into childhood summers. It wrapped him in the smell of his mother's apron and gentled him with the memory of his mother's embrace.

The woodcutter's heart slowed. His skin blued and marbled. The blood began to freeze in his veins.

Just before his heart stopped beating, Hulva kissed his eyelids and whispered to him, 'You took my children from me while they were sleeping. You took a knife to them and bladed the skin from their flesh. You burned their skin and enjoyed the warmth and the comforting smell of it. Then you chopped my children's flesh and chiselled it and turned it and smoothed it and grooved it. And now I will do the same to you.'

Hulva stretched her blood-blistered, razor-leaved branches towards the woodcutter. She scissored off his skin and cut out his heart. She stripped the flesh from his bones and sliced it into small pieces. Then she took the bones and the skin and she chiselled them and turned them and smoothed them and grooved them and made herself a throne from them.

She cooked his flesh over a fire and enjoyed the warmth and the righteous smell of it.

She took his boots, his axe and his heart and put them into his knapsack. She called a wolf and told it to take the knapsack to the woodcutter's cottage and leave it at the door.

⊳—◆⊷—○—◂◆—◁

When the moon was too full to move and the stars were bright enough to light the way to Heaven, the wind visited Hulva. The wind carried the sound of four breaking hearts into the clearing at the heart of the wood and shattered it all around the queen.

'What is this news, wind?' asked Hulva.

'This is the news of the woodcutter's family, Hulva. This is the news of how the woodcutter's wife opened the door of her cottage to welcome her husband home for supper and saw his knapsack all covered in blood.

'This is the news of how the woodcutter's wife took the knapsack and gave it to the woodcutter's mother to open because she was too afraid to open it herself.

'This is the news of how the woodcutter's children saw their father's boots come out of the knapsack, how the woodcutter's wife saw her husband's axe come out of the knapsack and how the woodcutter's mother lifted the heart of her own son out of the knapsack.'

Hulva laughed as she lowered herself on to her new throne of skin and bone. Her sharp voice cut bloody words into the night air. 'I like my throne, wind. Bring me more of Crann's sons.'

Hulva banshee-screamed the wind out of the woods and back to the village.

Verse 4

When the sun was too sleepy to grey the sky and the Angelus bell was loud enough to get lost in, the wind visited the church of Crann.

The church was full. The priest was sorrying a sad sermon for the woodcutter and his family. The woodcutter's mother was cradling her son's heart close to hers. Her heart was beating soft blessings of comfort to his, and the village was praying the woodcutter up to Heaven.

The wind carried the sound of Hulva's banshee-screaming into the cross of the church and howled it all around the priest.

'What is this news, wind?' asked the priest.

'This is the news of the demon in the wood that took the woodcutter, holy man. If you do not send your strongest men to kill the demon, it will surely come to your village and take you all.'

Three men with faces full of autumn but limbs full of spring, stood up from the front pew.

'We will go into the wood,' said the broadest of them.

'Then I shall show you the way,' said the wind.

The woodcutter's mother thanked the men, the priest blessed them and the rest of the villagers sent up the biggest prayers they could.

>·+·◆·-·O·-·◆·+·◄

The men swaddled themselves in furs, slung knapsacks across their backs and fetched their axes. The mothers of the village kissed their cheeks and stroked their heads. The fathers of the village nodded courage to them. The wives of the three men gentled them with their hands and tendered them with their eyes.

The men set off in the slow-falling snow. The wind blew gently enough to chime an icicle song. The men followed the icicle song into the wood.

As the men made their way into the wood, the snow stopped falling. Only their boots and their beating hearts were moving. Everything else was silent and slow-freezing still.

When the men reached the clearing at the heart of the wood, the icicle song stopped.

The men turned full-circle in search of the demon.

They saw Hulva's empty throne: the legs of it made from the woodcutter's polished thigh and shin bones, the seat of it made from his blue-marbled skin, the back of it made from his scoured ribs. His skinless hands reached out from the arm-bone armrests, and his head was still sitting on the bones of his shoulders, his rabbit-eyes staring straight at them.

The men's hearts thrashed in their chests, and their breath was so frightened that it froze. They readied their axes and waited for the demon.

The wind waited for Hulva to move. It waited for the men to fall and for the lullabying to start.

Hulva banshee-screamed and flailed up a snow storm with her scissor-branches. She snow-blinded the men until their eyes burned and they fell forward into the snow.

But this time, Hulva did not tell the younger holly to close their eyes and start to lullaby. The men did not drowsy, their hearts did not slow and the blood did not freeze in their veins. And when the terror in them was full awake, Hulva showed them no mercy.

She scissored off their skin and cut out their hearts. She butchered the flesh from their bones and sliced it into small pieces. She took the bones and the skin and chiselled them and turned them and smoothed them and grooved them and made herself three lanterns from them.

She set light to the pieces of flesh and put them into the lanterns and enjoyed the pale and pitiful dim of them.

She took their boots, axes and hearts and put them into the knapsacks. She called three wolves and told them to take the knapsacks to Crann and to leave them at the church door.

The younger holly cried for the men, but Hulva shushed and stilled them. Even the wind recoiled and howled with the horror of it.

'Quiet yourself, wind,' Hulva said. 'I have work for you. I like my lanterns. Bring me more of Crann's sons.'

Hulva chilled the wind out of the woods and back to the village.

⊱──◈──◈──⊰

The wind stilled itself in the churchyard and watched the priest find the knapsacks. The priest took out the boots and the axes and the hearts, and his toes curled up at the cruel of it and his own heart ached at the sad of it. And then he heavied the news to the homes of the three men.

The wind did not take any more of Crann's sons to Hulva that day, nor did it carry the news of the village to her.

Verse 5

When the moon was too beautiful not to sigh at and the sky was soft enough to sleep in, the wind visited Dara, the Oak King of the Banagher Glen.

Dara was big-handsome-strong and old-wise, and the wood he reigned over was wide and deep. In spring, hawthorn called up drifts of sweet primrose and bitter sorrel. In summer, rowan called in dragonflies. In autumn, ash called down sparrowhawks and buzzards, and in winter, oak called out deep-sleep prayers.

The wind carried the sound of the mourning village into the heart of the wood where Dara was sleeping and ached it all around him.

Dara woke up and asked, 'What is this news, wind?'

'This is the news of the village of Crann, Dara. The Holly Queen of Breen Wood is taking sons from the village and killing and cruelling them. If you do not stop her, she will surely take the whole village.'

The truth of the wind's words bit deep into Dara. He lifted his roots out of the ground and on to the snow and long-stepped it to Breen Wood, his powerful roots ploughing up the fields and his bare arms windmilling through the night sky.

When he got to the clearing at the heart of Breen Wood, the moon showed him Hulva's throne.

Then, Dara saw Hulva's lanterns: the shades made from the stretched skin of the men's faces, eyes shut tight and mouths open in a scream, the stands made from bloody leg-bones that looked like they were trying to run away. Inside each lantern smouldered a lump of human flesh.

Dara's roots curled up at the cruel of it.

Turning full-circle, Dara saw how the younger holly cowered and he heard their lonely lullabies, and his branches twisted at the sad of it.

When Hulva stepped into the clearing, Dara saw the sharp of her and the blood-blistered limbs of her, and his bark wrinkled at the horror of her.

'What business have you in my wood, old oak?' Hulva looked him up and down to see the make of him.

'I am Dara, the Oak King of the Banagher Glen, and I have come to ask you to stop your killing and cruelling.' Dara bowed himself and stretched out his branches towards Hulva.

'And I am Hulva, the Holly Queen of Breen Wood, and I will do what I want.' Hulva made herself tall and sharpened her leaves and pushed his bare branches away.

'Why have you done this, Hulva?' asked Dara.

'I am fairing-and-squaring with the village of Crann, Dara. They took my children from me, and now I am taking their children from them.' Hulva shook herself and her leaves scratched the air all about her.

'You ask me to stop, but I cannot. If I stop, they will come and take more of my children.' Hulva's roots shook at the thought of losing her children. They came loose and she fell over in the snow. Dara helped her upright and stretched his branches around her so that she could lean on him. He grew his roots into her roots so that he could listen to the story of her.

Underneath the hard of her, he could hear the hurt of her. Underneath the cruel of her, he could hear the fear of her. And underneath the hate of her, he could hear the love of her.

'I cannot lose another child, Dara,' said Hulva, her voice tired and full of heavy.

Dara curled his branches tighter around Hulva's. He lullabied her and called out deep-sleep prayers for her. As she slept, Dara sang heavenfuls of soothing songs to her until the bloody blisters on her branches healed. Then he gentled Hulva and couraged her and loved awake the forgiveness in her.

'If the villagers of Crann promise to take no more of your children, will you promise to take no more of theirs?' he asked.

Hulva watched the grey of the morning slink into the wood. She softened the sharp of her leaves and strengthened her roots and said, 'I will make that promise, Dara, but I ask that they bring my children back to the wood. In return, they may take their children back to Crann and holy them into the ground. That will be the end of the fairing-and-squaring.'

⊷⊶⊷○⊶⊷⊶

Dara long-stepped it to the village, furrowing deep tracks in the snow. He went straight to the church, reached a branch into the tower and rang the bell.

The priest was the first to appear and he trembled with fear when he saw Dara, all sky-tall and valley-wide.

'Are you the demon of the wood? Have you come to take us all?' The priest dropped to his knees, clasped his hands together and started Holy-Marying as fast as his lips could move.

'I am Dara, the Oak King of the Banagher Glen, and I am not a demon. I have come to speak the morning sermon. It will be full of soul comfort and good holy.'

The truth of Dara's words reached into the priest and Dara kept ringing the bell until the whole village came to the church. As the villagers arrived at the church doors, the priest welcomed them inside and told them that the Oak King was not a demon, but a holy messenger.

When the church was full, the priest closed the doors. Dara lifted the roof off the church and leaned in to sermon the people of Crann.

First, Dara sang heartfuls of swaddling songs to them until the wounds in their hearts healed. Then, Dara told them the story of Hulva and her children. He told them that Hulva was not a demon, but the Holly Queen of Breen Wood. He told them that she would stop taking the sons of Crann if they would stop taking her children, and he asked them to return her children to the wood and collect their own for holying into the ground.

At the end of the sermon, he gentled them and couraged them and loved the forgiveness deep into their souls.

When Dara had finished, the woodcutter's mother stood up from her pew and went to the cross of the church. She was carrying her son's heart, all wrapped in sweet cloths and blessed with big prayers. She put his heart to hers and said, 'Let us return Hulva's children to her, let us bring our own children home, and let there be peace between us.'

Every head in the church nodded. Every eye in the church cried. Every heart in the church beat bitter-sweet.

'Gather up Hulva's children and follow my tracks into the wood,' said Dara.

Then the Oak King put the roof back on to the church and long-stepped it back to the clearing at the heart of the wood.

Verse 6

The woodcutter's wife fetched the cradle, the blacksmith fetched the bowl, the priest and three good men fetched the church pew, and the coughing, crooked old man gripped the walking stick.

All the villagers swaddled themselves in furs and set off in the slow-falling snow. They followed Dara's tracks into the wood.

As the villagers made their way into the wood, the snow stopped falling. Only their boots and their beating hearts were moving. Everything else was silent and slow-freezing still.

When the villagers got to the clearing at the heart of the wood, the tracks stopped.

The villagers turned full-circle and saw the throne and the three lanterns.

Their toes curled up at the cruel of it and their hearts ached at the lonely-end of it all.

The mothers of the village gathered up the skin of the men. The fathers of the village gathered up the bones of the men. The wives of the men gentled the remains of them into four sacks that had been holied by the priest.

When they were done, the villagers moved to the edges of the clearing, and the woodcutter's mother called to Hulva, 'Holly Queen, we thank you for letting us take back the bodies of our children. As you asked, we have returned your children to the wood. May you know that we did not understand the hurt of taking them, and we are sore-sorry for the pain we caused you.'

Hulva lifted her roots out of the ground and moved to the

centre of the clearing. Her gaze fell on the coughing, crooked old man who was gripping on to the walking stick.

'Bring my hazel son to me, old man.'

The old man made a crooked bow to Hulva and said, 'Your son has been very kind to me, Holly Queen. He has walked with me and supported me and steadied my bones. Without him, I would not have been able to leave my home and visit my friends who lie in their graves. Without him, the heart in me would have lost its yearn for life.'

The old man lifted the walking stick and offered it to Hulva, but the stick jumped back to his side and said, 'Mother, the leaving of you was painful, but it did not kill me – the truth of it is that it was the making of me. I know you want me to return to the wood, but I want to stay with my old friend. He keeps me company and has never left me lonely.'

Although Hulva was hurt by her son's words, her heart was gladdened by his friendship with the old man.

><+>-0-<+><

Next, Hulva's gaze fell on the priest, who was sitting on the church pew.

'Bring my big oak son to me, holy man.'

The priest made a bow to Hulva and said, 'Your son has

shared his strength and his wisdom with our village. When we are heavy with woe, he carries us. When there is no one to hear our stories, he listens to us. And when grief has taken the words from us, he sends up wise and tender prayers for us. Without your son, our church would not be so holy.'

The priest called for the three good men to help him carry the pew to Hulva, but the pew pushed its feet into the snow and would not be lifted.

The pew said, 'Mother, the leaving of you was painful, but it did not kill me – the truth of it is that it was the making of me. I know you want me to return to the wood, but I want to stay with the priest and the village. I learn from the priest's words every day and when the villagers open their hearts to me, it warms me.'

Although Hulva was hurt by her son's words, she was proud of his wholesome heart.

⊱┄•◦•┄⊰

Then, Hulva's gaze fell on the blacksmith who was holding the bowl.

'Bring my birch daughter to me, young man.'

The blacksmith made a bow to Hulva and said, 'Your daughter has nourished my family to good health. She comforted hot broth into my bone-thin children until they were strong, and now she is feeding the child in my wife's belly.

Without her, my children would surely be dead. Without her, our unborn child may hunger itself up to Heaven.'

The blacksmith stretched out his arm and offered the bowl to Hulva, but the bowl leapt back to him and said, 'Mother, the leaving of you was painful, but it did not kill me – the truth of it is that it was the making of me. I know you want me to return to the wood, but I want to stay with the blacksmith's family. They fill me full every day and have never left me hungry.'

Although Hulva was hurt by her daughter's words, her heart was gladdened by the thriving of her once-sickly child.

▷┼◁▷┄○┄◁▷┼◁

Finally, Hulva's gaze fell on the woodcutter's wife who was standing next to the cradle.

'Bring my restless oak son to me, woman.'

The woodcutter's wife made a bow to Hulva and said, 'Your son has comforted and cosied both my children. He has rocked them in his arms, whispered gentle dreams to them and sweetened them with rest. Without your son, I would not have had a moment's sleep, and the weary of the wide-awake would have whittled me away.'

The woodcutter's wife bent down to lift the cradle to Hulva, but it started to rock so fast that she could not take a firm hold of it.

The cradle said, 'Mother, the leaving of you was painful,

but it did not kill me – the truth of it is that it was the making of me. I know you want me to return to the wood, but I want to stay with the woodcutter's family. They give me something precious to hold every day and thank me for my my restlessness.'

Although Hulva was hurt by her son's words, her heart was gladdened by the work that he had done in the woodcutter's home.

⊱─◦─◦─⊰

Hulva soft-leaved each of the villagers and said, 'I thought that you had killed and cruelled my children, but now I see that you have loved them and helped them to grow.'

Then, she soft-leaved the walking stick, the bowl, the pew and the cradle and said, 'You are free to return to the village of Crann. I see that you have loved the villagers and helped them to grow together.'

Next, Hulva tendered her branches around the necks of the four sacks, pulled them towards her trunk and said, 'Where are the hearts of these four men?'

The woodcutter's mother and the mothers of the three men who had faces full of autumn, but limbs full of spring, stepped forward. Each of them reached into their furs and pulled out their son's heart, all wrapped in sweet cloths and blessed with big prayers.

Hulva gentled her branches around the four hearts, put each of them into the right sack and said, 'Villagers of Crann, I have done you a great wrong and now I will fair-and-square with you.'

Cradling the sacks in her branches, Hulva cried all her sap on to them.

The sacks started to bulge and move until Hulva could no longer hold them.

The woodcutter and the three men who had faces full of autumn, but limbs full of spring, climbed out of the sacks. They all looked younger and stronger than before.

As the mothers of the four men opened their arms to embrace their sons, Hulva fell to the ground.

Dara wrapped his strong, bare branches around Hulva, grew his roots deep into hers and said, 'The Queen of Breen Wood is dying.'

The heart of the woodcutter's mother beat bitter-sweet. She rejoiced at the return of her own son, but she wept for the wood and its mother.

The woodcutter's mother went to Hulva, kneeled in the snow beside her and said, 'You have been a good mother and a noble queen. You have taught your children how to love and how to grow together. As the oldest mother of Crann, I promise you that our village will care for Breen Wood. We will love your children and keep them from harm. We will take only those who ask to come to Crann, and when their bodies break with old age, we will return them to Breen and plant the memory of them in the ground.'

Dara woke the sleeping wood and called in the wolves and the deer. He pulled the younger holly close and told the villagers to bring the walking stick, the pew, the bowl and the cradle to their mother.

As the whole wood sang the Song of Hulva, Dara planted the memory of her in the ground. He lay acorns all around her brittle limbs and kissed her and comforted her.

When he had finished planting the memory of her, Dara raised himself tall. He stood higher than any other tree in Breen Wood.

'I will not let Hulva lie in the ground on her own. I will lie with her and wrap my branches around her and gentle her until we are both made of earth.' As Dara spoke, his roots cut a deep trench in the ground. He lifted Hulva into the trench and then lay himself beside her. The ground covered them both up and soft-blanket-comforted them.

The priest went to the place where Hulva and Dara lay and gathered the villagers close. As the sons and daughters of Crann sang sad and soulful hymns, the priest holied the Holly Queen of Breen Wood and the Oak King of the Banagher Glen into the ground and made that place sacred.

When the snows melted, ten thousand acorns and ten thousand holly seeds sprang from that sacred place. The acorns and the holly seeds spread themselves around the wood and began to grow. The oak grew big-handsome-strong and old-wise. The holly grew old-beautiful and gentle-wise.

The oak and the holly took turns to watch over the wood. From the first wild garlic of the year until the harvest moon, the oak stood watch; from the harvest moon until the first wild garlic, the holly stood watch and lullabied the wood as it took its winter sleep.

The villagers visited the wood most every day and told the story of Hulva and Dara to the trees. The young mothers tidied around the trees and let their children play amongst the saplings. The older women tended the faerie wells and holy places. The old men kept the elderly trees company and listened to the wise of them, and the young men talked of travel and adventure with the younger trees.

If a tree from Breen asked to leave the wood, the woodcutter felled it with great care. When the woodcutter made a tree into a piece of furniture, he crafted it with deep holy and thankful respect. When the villagers took a piece of the woodcutter's furniture for their own, they loved it into the heart of their family.

Every year at the deepest dark, the holly wore blood-red berries to memory the blisters of their mother and the loss of her, and the villagers of Crann came to the sacred place at the heart of the wood to sing the Song of Hulva.

As the years passed, the love between the people of Crann and Breen Wood grew deep-root strong, and they all flourished and grew.

Verse 7

When the sun was too bold to hide itself and the blossom was sweet enough to get drunk on, the wind visited Crann. The wind carried the sound of marching men right into the heart of the village and beat it all around the tiny cottages.

'What is this news, wind?' asked the villagers.

'This is the news of an outlander army, Crann. They have come to take the trees from Breen Wood and make them into ships, and they have come to take your furniture to sell for gold. They will cut down any man who stands in their way.'

As the villagers raised arms to fight the army, the wind carried the news into the heart of the wood, to the sacred place where Hulva and Dara were buried.

The wind blew the news hard into the ground.

The wind blew so hard that it blew the breath back into Hulva and Dara.

The wind blew so hard that it blew the shine back into the stars that had fallen to the ground.

The mother star lifted her child into the sky and they both shone into the eyes of the outlander army until it was blinded.

Hulva stretched her branches out to the village and took it into the wood, then she fast-grew a high, thick hedge all around it. The hedge was so sharp that it would have cut the life out of anyone who tried to get through it.

Dara stretched out his roots until they reached the faerie hill at Tieveragh. The faeries travelled to Breen Wood on his roots and magicked the wood and the villagers safe from all outsiders.

When the wood and the villagers were all cosied in, Hulva and Dara returned to the ground, and the mother star and her child rose back up into the night sky to shine down on Breen Wood.

>-◄0-0-◄0-┤-◄

The villagers and the trees lived happily together inside Breen Wood for many years. When the last villager died, the sharp holly hedge softened and let outsiders in so that the trees had company, but if anyone tried to cruel a tree or take it against its will, the faeries made sure that the people were bad-lucked for ever.

Breen Wood still stands to this day, and if you visit it between the time of the first wild garlic and the harvest moon, you will see the oak keeping watch. And if you visit it at the deepest dark, you will see the holly wearing their blood-red berries in memory of their mother. And if the wind is still, you may even hear them lullabying the wood as it takes its winter sleep.

And if you visit the wood at night, be sure to look up, won't you? Most everyone says that those two stars are still there, and that they will shine as long as Breen Wood stays standing.

The SPIRIT of the MEADOW BURN

The Water Wheel

Not in your time, not in my time, but in the time when the rivers spilled magick and the wind blew secrets, there was a farmer and his wife who lived a short gallop from the village of Bushmills. They were good, hard-working people and had two fine sons. Their elder son was called Asriel and their younger son was called Ezekiel.

When the farmer and his wife became too old to work the ground, Asriel took a wife of his own. The two brothers worked the ground together and Asriel's wife worked stone-hard to look after the farmhouse and the old farmer and his wife. But the farm was not big enough to feed five mouths, so Ezekiel took work in a corn mill on the banks of the River Bush.

Every day, Ezekiel worked from before sunrise until after sunset. At the beginning of the day, it was his job to clear the headrace and the water wheel before opening the sluice gates. At the end of the day, it was his job to close the sluice gates to stop the wheel that drove the millstone. In between, he ground the grain, filled sacks and fixed anything that broke.

The old miller was pleased to have such a healthy young man in his employ: Ezekiel had legs as solid as ground-stone gate posts, hands as big as shovels and a back as broad as a barn door. People said that he could lift the millstone with his bare hands, that he could push harder than the full-spate current of the River Bush and that he could pull more weight than a team of well-fed oxen.

>-+-+>-0-<+-+-<

One dark spectre of a morning, when the fog was choking the sky and the frost was cowering at every door, Ezekiel set off for the mill. As usual, he was the first to arrive and he set about his tasks without delay. Taking a lantern to inspect the headrace and the water wheel, he could see that the blazing, autumn wind had blown in a mulch of leaves and a rickle of branches.

He climbed into the headrace and shovelled out the leaves and branches with one hand while he held on to the lantern with the other, just as he had done a hundred times before. Then he reached into the water wheel to clean it out, just as he had done a hundred times before. But this time, unlike any of the before times, Ezekiel lost his balance and fell on to the wheel, and the heft of him pulled the wheel forwards and into the icy, black water.

When the wheel stopped, Ezekiel found himself upside-down and dip-dunked in right over his head. The light in his lantern had been swallowed up by the river, and in the tar-pitch black of it, poor Ezekiel tried to free himself from the wheel. But the more he struggled to free himself, the more he got himself caught in it.

When the breath was nearly full out of him, and the water was leaking into him, Ezekiel started to send up big help-me prayers. If no one opened the sluice gates, then the headrace would not fill with water and the wheel would not turn and bring him up for air. It would be a good long time before anyone else would be at the mill, and, if his prayers were not answered swiftly, Ezekiel knew that his life would surely come to a full stop.

Then, just as his heart was starting to slow-beat out its own sorry requiem, Ezekiel noticed a strange light in the dark water. A shimmer of silver stars danced and dived their way towards him, and, when they were right upon him, they exploded like a huge, silent firework.

The light was so bright that Ezekiel took it for the big shine of Heaven. He closed his eyes and started saying his goodbyes to the earthly world, but his goodbyeing was interrupted by a mighty shaking and a grim gowl of a howl.

Ezekiel opened his eyes to find a little fish-man shoulder-shaking him. The fish-man was only as tall as a short man's shank. Instead of legs, he had a pair of scaly, flint-grey fishtails, and instead of hands, shiny lobster claws. His roaring-rufous beard swirled about his water-wrinkled face, and his head seemed to be bigger than the rest of his body put together.

'Breathe! Breathe! Breathe! Please! Please! Please!' begged the little fish-man as he big-cheeked his face and blew a bubble of air around Ezekiel's head.

Ezekiel sucked in a lungful of air and cried, 'I am breathing, sir. My prayers have been answered. I must know whom I am to thank for the saving of me – what is your name?'

The little fish-man looked mighty relieved to see that Ezekiel was still alive. He blew out a pearl-string of bubbles, ear-to-eared a smile and answered, 'I am Breewa, the water spirit of the Meadow Burn. I am sorry to say that your prayers have *not* been answered – but mine have. I did not come to save you. I came to get your body so I could take it to the faeries. They won't take a dead body, see, only a live one. And they only take big, strong, healthy ones. I'd say that the faeries will pay me treasurous well for a body like yours. Today, sir, you will make me rich, so it is me who should be thanking you.' Breewa whirled and gurgled with glee. 'And to think I only came to the Bush to catch me a salmon for my supper. Look what I caught instead!'

'What will they do with my body, Breewa?' asked Ezekiel, the worry worming itself between his ears.

'They will cut the soul out of you like this.' Breewa click-clacked his claws all around the edges of Ezekiel and pretended to heave-ho the poor man's soul out of him.

'And then they will put a faerie inside your handsome body like this.' Breewa held the sharp of his claws against Ezekiel's forehead and pushed hard enough to draw blood.

'And what will happen to my soul?' asked Ezekiel, the blood

treacle-trickling from his brow into his eyes.

'It will wander, sir,' said Breewa.

'And what will the faerie do when he is in my body?' asked Ezekiel.

'He will do whatever he likes, sir,' chuckled Breewa.

Ezekiel did not like the thought of his soul wandering around without a body, nor did he want a faerie living in his skin. His eyes watered up with the sad of it all.

When Breewa saw that Ezekiel was tearsying up, the little fish-man started to tearsy up too, and said, 'I cannot bear to see you so sad, sir. I tell you what I'll do – I'll set you four tasks. If you complete them all succesfully, then you may keep your body and your life – and I'd wager that you are big enough, and strong enough, to easy-breezy your way through them. But if you fail any of the tasks, then I will have to take you straight to the faeries. Now, I can't say fairer than that, can I?'

When Ezekiel heard Breewa's offer, he was dance-a-jig happy and said, 'Well, that is fairer than the fairest thing I have ever heard. Let me at the first task.'

The Tasks

Breewa freed Ezekiel from the water wheel and put him in a

golden, tight-meshed net. The net was as small as a minnow on the outside but as big as a whale on the inside, and Ezekiel tumbled around in it as Breewa flip-tailed his way up the river.

When Breewa got to the Conogher ford, he sprang out of the water and slapped his net on to the ground. He opened the mouth of the net and emptied Ezekiel out into a big, flat field.

A winter-white raven with summer-sea eyes circled above them.

'Now stand you up tall, sir, and I'll call my friend,' said Breewa.

The water spirit whistled and something the size and shape of a hungry cat dropped out of a nearby tree. From all fours, it raised itself feebly onto its bony back legs. It was covered in a thin, blue-grey skin that was so tight that you could see its insides, and there wasn't a single hair on its body. It had a small slit of a mouth and cataract-clouded eyes that seemed to rearrange themselves every time Ezekiel blinked.

'This is Smeench,' announced Breewa. Smeench bowed, but said nothing.

'I am Ezekiel, and I am pleased to make your acquaintance, sir,' polited Ezekiel as he bowed in return.

'For the first task, you must run a race against poor little Smeench and win. All you have to do is sprint the length of the field and back. Easy-breezy, sir,' said Breewa, winking at Ezekiel.

When Ezekiel heard Breewa's words, he fair popped with please. Ezekiel was a blister-fast runner, and he could cover the length of a field in fewer than three strides. He was certain that he would beat this poor little creature.

Breewa click-clacked his claws and the race started, but Ezekiel had not even taken his first stride before Smeench had blurred his way to the end of the field and back.

'Well, what a surprise, sir! You have been bested by Smeench, and now I must take you to the faeries.' Breewa shook his head and sighed as though he had never seen a sadder sight.

Even though Ezekiel was dazed by his defeat, he tried to quick-wit his way out of trouble. He turned on his tears and cried, 'Oh, Breewa! I do not want to go to the faeries. I will give you my Sunday-best coat if you give me another chance.'

Breewa tearsy'd up and said, 'I cannot bear to see you so sad, sir. I will gladly give you another chance. In fact, so rightly am I tendering to your plight that if you complete the next task succesfully, then you will keep your body, your life and your Sunday-best coat. But if you are not successful, then you will give me your coat, and I will take you straight to the faeries. Now, I can't say fairer than that, can I?'

When Ezekiel heard Breewa's offer, he was dance-a-jig

happy and said, 'Well, that is fairer than the fairest thing I have ever heard. Let me at the second task.'

⊱•⊰

Breewa put Ezekiel back into the net, and Ezekiel tumbled around in it as Breewa flip-tailed his way further up the river.

When Breewa got to the Stranocum ford, he sprang out of the water and slapped his net on to the ground. He opened the mouth of the net and emptied Ezekiel on to a bench set at a table laden with feasting food. Next to this stood an identical bench and table, also laden with feasting food.

A winter-white raven with summer-sea eyes circled above them.

'You must be hungry after your race with Smeench. Now, sit yourself comfy, sir, and I'll call you some company,' said Breewa.

The water spirit whistled and a thin, hot-cheeked boy stepped out from behind a gorse bush. He looked like he'd seen no more than seven harvests. Truth be told, it looked like he'd not see the next – he was all dripping with the fever, and his clothes were stuck to his clammy body.

'This is Lusk,' announced Breewa. Lusk bowed, but said nothing.

'I am Ezekiel, and I am pleased to make your acquaintance,

young sir,' polited Ezekiel as he bowed in return.

'For the second task, all you have to do is eat more than poor little Lusk. Easy-breezy, sir,' said Breewa, winking at Ezekiel.

When Ezekiel heard Breewa's words, he fair popped with please. Ezekiel had the appetite of a bear, and he could eat three whole pigs in one sitting. He was certain that he could eat more than this poor little boy.

Lusk sat at the table next to Ezekiel's, and they gazed at the food laid out before them. Heads of boar with apple-stuffed jaws were squeezed between silver-beaked peacocks and drape-necked swans. Shimmering sides of salmon were piled up next to juicy jugged hares and spicy spatch-cocked blackbirds. Honey dripped from oven-warm loaves, and rounds of cheese lined the edges of the table. By the time Breewa click-clacked his claws to signal the start of the eating, Ezekiel's mouth was fair drookit with the drool.

Ezekiel ploughed his way through three loaves, two rounds of cheese, five blackbirds and a whole head of boar – ears, snout and all. Feeling terrible tight at the seams, and almost halfway through the food on his table, he lifted his head from his trencher to see how Lusk was faring.

Ezekiel was astonished to see that Lusk had not only eaten all the food on his table, but he had eaten the table itself, the trenchers and the bench too.

'Well, what a surprise, sir! You have been bested by Lusk,

and now I must take you to the faeries.' Breewa shook his head and sighed as though he had never seen a sadder sight.

Again, Ezekiel tried to quick-wit his way out of trouble. He turned on his tears and cried, 'Oh, Breewa! I do not want to go to the faeries. I will give you my pocket watch if you give me another chance.'

Breewa tearsy'd up and said, 'I cannot bear to see you so sad, sir, and I will gladly give you another chance. In fact, so rightly am I tendering to your plight that if you complete the next task successfully, then you will keep your body, your life, your Sunday-best coat and your pocket watch. But if you are not successful, then you will give me your coat and your watch, and I will take you straight to the faeries. Now, I can't say fairer than that, can I?'

When Ezekiel heard Breewa's offer, he was dance-a-jig happy and said, 'Well, that is fairer than the fairest thing I have ever heard. Let me at the third task.'

><+>-0-<+><

Breewa put Ezekiel back into the net, and Ezekiel tumbled around in it as Breewa flip-tailed his way further up the river.

When Breewa got to the stepping stones at Clontyfinnan, he sprang out of the water and slapped his net on to the ground. He opened the mouth of the net and emptied Ezekiel out on to one of the stepping stones.

A winter-white raven with summer-sea eyes circled above them.

'You must be mighty thirsty after all your feasting. Now, wait you a moment, sir, and I'll get you a drink,' said Breewa.

Breewa reached into the river and pulled out a drinking horn that was lipped all around in silver.

'For the third task, all you have to do is drink the horn dry. Easy-breezy, sir,' said Breewa, winking at Ezekiel.

When Ezekiel heard Breewa's words, he fair popped with please. Ezekiel's mouth was tinder-dry, and he had a reputation for being able to empty a drinking horn in a single gulp. He was certain that he could drink this horn dry.

Ezekiel took the horn from Breewa and lifted it to his lips. The horn was so long that the tip of it touched the water, and so full that it was overflowing, but there was not even a tiny tremble of the worriment in him.

By the time Breewa click-clacked his claws to signal the start of the drinking, Ezekiel's mouth was fair gasping with the thirst. He gulped and gulped until he was so full of water that it was spilling out of his ears and his nose, but when he looked into the horn to see how he was faring, it was still half full.

In spite of his dismay, Ezekiel took the horn to his mouth again and gulped and gulped until he was so full of water that it was running out of the ends of his fingers and his toes, but when he looked into the horn to see how he was faring, it was still a third full.

As Breewa looked into the horn, Ezekiel dropped his head in defeat.

'Well, what a surprise, sir! You have been bested by the horn, and now I must take you to the faeries.' Breewa shook his head and sighed as though he had never seen a sadder sight.

Once again, Ezekiel tried to quick-wit his way out of trouble. He turned on his tears and cried, 'Oh, Breewa! I do not want to go to the faeries. I will give you my horse if you give me another chance.'

Breewa tearsy'd up and said, 'I cannot bear to see you so sad, sir, and I will gladly give you another chance. In fact, so rightly am I tendering to your plight that if you complete the next task successfully, then you will keep your body, your life, your Sunday-best coat, your pocket watch and your horse. But if you are not successful, then you will give me your coat, your watch and your horse, and I will take you straight to the faeries. Now, I can't say fairer than that, can I?'

When Ezekiel heard Breewa's offer, he was dance-a-jig happy and said, 'Well, that is fairer than the fairest thing I have ever heard. Let me at the fourth task.'

➤┅❖┅०┅❖┅┅

Breewa put Ezekiel back into the net, and Ezekiel tumbled around in it as Breewa flip-tailed his way right back down the river and out into the Meadow Burn.

When Breewa got to Ballyness, he sprang out of the water and slapped his net on to the ground. He opened the mouth of the net and emptied Ezekiel out into a small woodland clearing by the banks of the burn.

A winter-white raven with summer-sea eyes circled above.

'You must be itching for a good fight after all your eating and drinking. Now, wait you a moment, sir, and I'll get you someone to wrestle with,' said Breewa.

The water spirit whistled and a little old woman shuffled out from behind an ash tree. She had a crickit-crookit nose that reached down to her chin, her ruckled face was all hairy-warted, and her teeth had long since rotted out of her gums. She looked like she'd seen more than seven hundred harvests. Truth be told, it looked like she'd not see the next – she was all twisted up with the bone sickness and looked like she would crumble to dust at the slightest touch.

'This is Shan,' announced Breewa. Shan creaked a shallow bow, but said nothing.

'I am Ezekiel, and I am pleased to make your acquaintance, madam,' polited Ezekiel as he bowed in return.

'For the fourth task, all you have to do is beat poor little Shan in a wrestling match. Easy-breezy, sir,' said Breewa, winking at Ezekiel.

When Ezekiel heard Breewa's words, he did not pop with please. Ezekiel was a big, strong heft of a man, and he could wrestle a bull into submission with one bare hand. He was certain that he could beat this poor little old woman, but he did not want to harm her.

'This is a devil-dark task, Breewa. I will surely win, and Shan will surely die,' said Ezekiel.

'If you do not fight her, you cannot win, and if you do not win, I must take you to the faeries,' warned Breewa. 'Do what you will, sir.'

Although Ezekiel was not best pleased about it, he came to the conclusion that he had no choice but to wrestle with Shan.

>—·—◆—·—◇—·—<

Breewa click-clacked his claws to signal the start of the wrestling. Ezekiel asked Shan to forgive him and then he charged his full weight into her, but she did not move. Not an inch did she drift. Her twisted bones refused to shift.

Unwilling to surrender, Ezekiel hauled up a dogged determination from the bottom of his boots and used the ferocious force of it to grapple with Shan. He pushed and he pulled, he tugged and he tore, he pleaded and he prayed, and he cursed and swore, but Shan used her skill and stayed stock-still.

Ezekiel was all wobblit-weary, but he would not give up. He staggered back a pace or two, and then he hurled his exhausted body into Shan once more. This time, when Ezekiel was right upon her, Shan put her reed-thin arms around him. She cosied and tendered him as if he were her own son, and then she pushed him to the ground as easy as you like, resting one bony foot on his back to show her victory.

'Well, what a surprise, sir! You have been bested by Shan, and now I must take you to the faeries.' Breewa shook his head and sighed as though he had never seen a sadder sight.

This time, Ezekiel tearsy'd up for real, and he cried, 'Oh, Breewa! I do not want to go to the faeries, but I have nothing left to offer you. What can I do to save myself?'

But Breewa did not tearsy up as he had before. Instead, he filled his voice with frost and said, 'There is nothing you can do to save yourself. I have been fair with you but you have failed all four of my tasks. Now you will give me your Sunday-best coat, your pocket watch and your horse, and I will take you to the faeries.'

Just as Breewa was about to push Ezekiel into his net, the winter-white raven that had been circling above them swept down to the ground and turned itself into the most beautiful woman that Ezekiel had ever seen.

Her hair was as white as milk and as long as for ever. Her skin was as fresh as April, and her summer-sea eyes spun sparkling stars into the air about her. She was as lithe as a willow, and she had the smell of soft, sweet slumber all about her.

Breewa flopped to the floor and planted his nose into the ground. Without looking up, he grabbed Ezekiel's legs and pulled him to the ground too.

'Bow, you fool!' whispered Breewa, his fishtail feet twitchit-trembling and his lobster claws chitter-chattering. 'That is Alva, the most powerful faerie in these parts.'

Alva stepped towards Ezekiel, bent down and took his face in her hands.

'Breewa has not been fair with you at all, Ezekiel,' said Alva, her words hanging like a dream in the air between them. 'Truth be told, what he has done to you is unfairer than the unfairest thing I have ever seen. You have been tricked.'

The Pot Still

Alva froze the world lifeless still about Ezekiel: the burn stopped babbling, the wind stopped whispering, and Breewa's claws stopped chitter-chattering.

As Alva began to speak, Ezekiel wondered at the full misty magick of her.

'The tasks you undertook were not what they seemed,'

she explained. 'You did not run a race against a creature called Smeench but against Thought. No mortal can run faster than Thought.'

'Well, that was crookit-crafty,' said Ezekiel.

'You did not lose the eating contest to a boy called Lusk but to Wild Fire. No mortal can eat as much, or as quickly, as Wild Fire,' she continued.

'Well, that was sneakit-sly,' said Ezekiel.

'The tip of your drinking horn was not closed but open. Breewa magicked the tip of the horn into Lough Neagh. No mortal can drink a whole lough.'

'Well, that was griftit-guileful,' said Ezekiel.

'And you did not wrestle with an old woman called Shan but against Old Age. No mortal can beat Old Age.'

'Well, that was wickit-wily,' said Ezekiel.

'He tricked you out of all your possessions, and you stood not a chip of a chance of keeping your body. That was not fair, Ezekiel, and the faerie folk are unshakeable firm about the fairness of things. Because Breewa did not take you fairly, the faeries will not take your body from you – in fact, you can take his. Now, I can't say fairer than that, can I?' Alva raised her hands and magicked Breewa off the ground and into his own net. When he was safe inside, she magicked everything moving again, smalled the net right down and gave it to Ezekiel.

'Well, that is fairer than the fairest thing I have ever heard, but what use have I for a water spirit?' asked Ezekiel, the net writhing in his hands.

'Within seven years, Breewa will make you a very rich man. Go home to the farm and empty Breewa into your pot still. Enjoy the whiskey that comes from the still, but share it only with your family. When the time is right, I will visit you and tell you what to do. In the meantime, tell no one of this.'

>─+‹•›─0─‹•›+‹

Ezekiel did exactly as Alva had said. He went home and put the water spirit into the pot still. He told no one of Breewa or Alva, but he told everyone that he had been good-luck-charmed when he fell into the water wheel at the mill, that the wheel had dropped him into the tailrace and that the river had safe-and-sounded him up into the Meadow Burn.

The old miller was happy that the river had returned Ezekiel: Ezekiel continued to work break-your-back hard at the corn mill.

Asriel and his wife were happy that the river had returned Ezekiel: the belly of Asriel's wife was bursting ripe, and Ezekiel continued to help with the feeding of a growing family.

Ezekiel's old parents were happy that the river had returned Ezekiel: Ezekiel continued to be a kind and loving son.

>─+‹•›─0─‹•›+‹

Almost seven years passed, and, had it not been for the whiskey in his pot still, Ezekiel might have forgotten all about Breewa and Alva. The still clitter-clattered day and night with Breewa's kicking and complaining. The first time that Ezekiel's family heard the clamour, Ezekiel said that Asriel's barley was fair spry and that the noise was just the sound of vigorous distilling. Ezekiel praised his brother for his growing gift, and Asriel was well pleased.

Even though the clamour continued year after year, Ezekiel's family never asked about the noise again. They simply enjoyed the delicious dew that dripped from the swan-necked still. The whiskey from it was summer-meadow sweet and full of the lively.

But, while Ezekiel's still was producing good whiskey, it was not the same for the stills on other farms, or for the distilleries in Bushmills. The day Ezekiel emptied Breewa into his pot still, their stills soured, and no matter which water or grain they used, the whiskey was only good for spitting out. And while everyone else bleated and brawled about the lack of good whiskey, Ezekiel told his family to keep the still on their farm a secret.

'If folk hear news of our good whiskey, they will surely come and steal our still. They may even kill us to get a dram from it,' warned Ezekiel.

Ezekiel's family stayed silent.

Exactly one moon before the seven years were up, Ezekiel was clip-clopping his way home from the corn mill when a winter-white raven with summer-sea eyes swooped out of the night sky and on to the ground in front of his horse.

'Is that you, Alva?' asked Ezekiel.

'It is, Ezekiel,' answered Alva, turning herself into her full faerie form. She was even more beautiful than Ezekiel remembered. His heart flitter-fluttered at the sight of her, his cheeks flushed with blush at the smell of her, and his ears gladdened at the bewitch of her voice.

Ezekiel bowed his head and welcomed her with his eyes.

'I have been watching you these past seven years, and you have done exactly as I said. Now I have come to tell you what to do next. Do exactly as I say, and within seven days, Breewa will make you a very rich man.'

Alva told Ezekiel what to do next. When she had finished, she turned herself back into the winter-white raven and flew off into the night.

The Test

On the seventh day after Alva had visited him, Ezekiel clip-clopped his way home from the corn mill. When he got to the farmhouse, he scrubbed himself clean and put on his Sunday-best coat.

He asked Asriel's wife to set five extra places at the table and to lay out plenty of bread and cheese. He asked Asriel to stoke up the hearth with peats. He told his family that guests would come that evening and that he would be heartful happy if they would good-company the guests as best they could.

At seven o'clock, there was a knock on the door and Ezekiel opened it. In front of him stood five men. Above the five men circled a winter-white raven with summer-sea eyes.

Ezekiel made a courteous bow and said, 'I am honoured to welcome you. Please come in and take a seat at the table, gentlemen. And, raven, you come in too.'

The five men and the winter-white raven went into the farmhouse.

Asriel's wife scattered crumbs on the floor for the raven and cut cheese and bread for the men.

When everyone was seated at the table, the oldest of the five men said, 'We thank you for your invitation, and we are rightly looking forward to your ... *hospitality*.' The oldest, the youngest, the fattest and the thinnest of the five men all smiled big know-a-secret smiles, licked their lips and winked, but the quietest of the men showed nothing on his face and kept his counsel.

Asriel's wife took her own meaning from the guests' faces

and made sure that their trenchers were kept piled high with food.

Asriel also took his own meaning from the guests' faces and made sure that the fire burned constant-cosy-warm.

And Ezekiel's old parents took their own meaning from the guests' faces, too, and filled the air with old-time stories about how the sky was made.

When the five men had taken their fill of food, the youngest of them looked at Ezekiel and said, 'And now for the hospitality, sir?'

Well, Asriel and his wife and Ezekiel's parents were mighty perplexed by the young man's words. Asriel's wife put her hands on her hips, furrowed her brow and opened her mouth to rip-roar at the man's rudeness, but Ezekiel raised his hand and stood up from his chair.

'Fetch a fresh jar of whiskey from the still, Asriel,' said Ezekiel, nodding and winking at each of the men in turn.

Ezekiel's words made Asriel's eyes fair shoot out of his head. Asriel's wife crumpled into a lost-for-words swoon on the floor, and Ezekiel's parents sucked in a whole gust of air and blustered out a Lord-Save-Us prayer.

Ezekiel laughed and said, 'Don't worry. They have not come to steal our still, nor have they come to kill us for a dram. These are honourable men, one from each of the letter-of-the-law distilleries in Bushmills. If they like the whiskey, they will offer a handsome price for the still.'

▸┄◈┄○┄◈┄◂

Asriel brought a jar of whiskey to the table, and Ezekiel filled five small cups with the lively liquid.

The oldest of the five men drank first and said, 'That is the finest whiskey I have ever tasted, and I will make you an offer of twenty pots of gold for your still.'

The youngest of the five men drank second and said, 'That is the finest whiskey I have ever tasted, and I will make you an offer of thirty pots of gold for your still.'

The fattest of the five men drank third and said, 'That is the finest whiskey I have ever tasted, and I will make you an offer of forty pots of gold for your still.'

The thinnest of the five men drank fourth and said, 'That is the finest whiskey I have ever tasted, and I will make you an offer of fifty pots of gold for your still.'

The quietest of the five men drank last and said, 'That is indeed the finest whiskey I have ever tasted, but I am not rich enough to offer you its full worth. Fifty pots of gold is a fair offer, but I have only ten pots of gold to my name. I will give you all my gold in exchange for your still.'

Every eye in Ezekiel's family was fixed on the thinnest of the five men, but Ezekiel said nothing. Instead, he turned to the winter-white raven and nodded his head.

The raven circled once above the five men and landed on the shoulder of the quietest man.

Ezekiel bowed to the men and said, 'You are all honourable men and you have made me five good offers. Any of those offers would make me a very rich man and give a good life to me and my family. I have decided to accept the lowest offer.'

Ezekiel's family stood wide-open-mouthed and wordless at Ezekiel's decision. The oldest, the youngest, the fattest and the thinnest of the five men scratched their heads in disbelief and let out loud well-I-never sighs.

The quietest of the five men showed nothing on his face and said, 'This is good news, sir, and I thank you for accepting my offer. To show my gratitude, I will make sure that this farm receives a supply of whiskey from your still for as long as the distillery stands.'

Ezekiel and the quietest of the five men shook hands. Ezekiel and Asriel loaded the pot still onto the quietest man's cart. The quietest man unloaded ten pots of gold from his cart and carried them into the farmhouse.

The five distillery men drove off into the night. The winter-white raven close-followed the quietest of the five men with the pot still in his cart. Ezekiel closed the farmhouse door.

'But why did you not take the fifty pots of gold?' asked Ezekiel's old mother as soon as the door was closed.

'Even with ten pots of gold, I am a very rich man, and you

will all benefit from my wealth,' answered Ezekiel. 'The pot still has gone to the right man – of that I am sure.'

The Best-Kept Secret

When the quietest of the five distillery men was well on his way home, Alva turned herself from a raven into her full faerie form and walked out in front of his cart.

He pulled up his horses hard so that he would not hurt Alva.

'I did not see you, madam. I am sorry for nearly hurting you,' said the quietest man.

'You would not have hurt me, Hugh. And I do not let myself be seen by many people,' said Alva.

'How do you know my name?' asked the quietest man.

'I have been watching you. The pot still is yours because you were willing to give everything you had for it and because I have seen that you can keep a secret. You are a quiet man, and you show nothing on your face,' explained Alva as she climbed onto the cart beside Hugh. 'Now drive on to your distillery, and I will tell you the secret that you must keep.'

As Hugh drove onwards to Bushmills, Alva told him all about Breewa and how the lively spirit flavoured the water and made good whiskey. She told him that the whiskey all about Bushmills had soured because Breewa no longer lived in the Meadow Burn nor fished for salmon in the River Bush. She told him how Ezekiel had come to own Breewa and how Ezekiel had kept the secret of the still for seven years.

'And now it is your turn to keep the secret, Hugh. If you keep the secret of the still, then you will become a very rich man. No other pot still or distillery will make whiskey that is as meadow-sweet or as full of the lively because the water they use will have no spirit in it. But if you don't keep the secret, it is certain that folk will try to steal Breewa and your still,' said Alva.

'But how will I keep the secret? What will I say when people ask me why my whiskey tastes better than anyone else's?' puzzled Hugh.

'That is easy. You will tell people that Saint Columba came to you in a dream and told you that he had once blessed the part of the Meadow Burn on which your distillery sits. You will tell them that the saint looked down from Heaven, and when he saw that there was not a single good dram to be had in Bushmills, he revived his old blessing to sweeten your whiskey. No one will doubt it, Hugh. Nor will anyone try to steal the holy blessing for themselves, because everyone knows that stolen blessings don't work. You and your distillery will be left in peace, and the secret of the still will stay safe.'

Hugh nodded, and Alva turned herself back into a winter-white raven and flew off into the night.

>⸱⊷⸱○⸱⊶⸱<

Alva chose well – Hugh kept the secret. In fact, he went as far as to call for the renaming of the Meadow Burn in honour of Saint Columba's blessing. The Meadow Burn became Saint Columb's Rill, Hugh became a very rich man and the secret of the still has been kept to this very day.

As for Ezekiel, the morning after the deal for the still was done, he went to the corn mill and asked the old miller if he would sell the mill and his stock to him.

The old miller was worn out with work and said, 'You have worked break-your-back hard for me for seven years. I would be happy to sell it to you for seven pots of gold.'

Ezekiel shook hands with the old miller and then went to the church and asked the minister if he could buy the best burial plot for his family.

The minister said, 'I would be happy to sell you the best plot for a single pot of gold.'

Ezekiel shook hands with the minister and then went home to the farm.

When the whole family was around the table that evening,

Ezekiel said, 'Asriel, I have bought you the corn mill: may it keep your belly full and your children's children in good health.'

Next, he turned to his old parents and said, 'Mother and Father, I have bought our family the best burial plot in the church grounds: may we all lie together when the time comes.'

Then, Ezekiel lifted a pot of gold on to the table and said, 'And this gold is for unforeseen happenings: may you never worry about the future again.'

The whole family was easy-heart happy at Ezekiel's news but soon saddened when Ezekiel said, 'And with this last pot of gold, I am away to America to find myself a wife.'

>-+◦>-○-◦>-+-◦

What happened next, nobody knows for sure. There are some people who say that Ezekiel did leave for America with a pot of gold and that he found himself a pretty wife and lived a good, long life.

There are other people who say that he went to Canada with his pot of gold and lumber-jacked and logged for the love of it but never found a wife. These people say that his pot of gold was a magick pot that never emptied and that, just before he died, he put the pot into the Klondike River and started a rumour that grew into the Gold Rush.

But most people say that Ezekiel left for neither America nor Canada, but stayed and married the most beautiful woman that anyone had ever seen. They say that her hair was as white as milk and as long as for ever. They say that her skin was as fresh as April and that her summer-sea eyes spun sparkling stars into the air. They say that she was as lithe as a willow and that she had the smell of soft, sweet slumber all about her.

And they say that the day Ezekiel married her, he disappeared and never returned – not even to lie in his own grave.

The TERRIBLE TALE of
FILLAN McQUILLAN

Salvation

High up on the Lannimore Hill, looking out over the Giant's Cut and across to Rathlin Island, there once stood a big white house. When the house was not three years built, the owner was minded to make a new life for himself in America, so he put up the house for auction. Most every wealthy local man put in a generous bid for the big white house, but a stranger called Fillan McQuillan outbid them all.

When Fillan McQuillan arrived on the Lannimore Hill, he stirred a whisper that raced the length of the coast from Colliery Bay to Portballintrae and a fair way inland too. There were rumours of a drove of high-tailed Arabian horses, of cartloads of fine furniture and of precious ornaments wrapped in Chinese silk. There was no mention of a wife or children or where the man had come from, but there was plenty of talk about how he had the air of the holy about him. It was not a welcoming holy, but it was a kind of holy all the same.

Fillan McQuillan lost no time in making himself known to all sorts of company. Dressed in a long, black coat and a wide-brimmed hat in the Roman style, he rode out from his house and knocked on the doors of dwellings big and small.

When people opened the door to him, they would take him for a priest and welcome him in.

'Well, Father,' they would say, 'we didn't know that we were getting a new priest!'

And then Fillan McQuillan would holy his bony hands together, tilt his head to one side and say, 'I am not a priest, but I have been called to this place by God Himself to do His most important work – work that no priest can do.'

Then the curious would grow big in people, and they would ask, 'And might we know the nature of this work?'

And then Fillan McQuillan would cast his arms wide and roll his eyes back into his head and shake from top to toe. And then, in a mysterious voice that would rattle the very bones of you and make you want to kneel right down and pray, he would boom, 'God Himself has called Fillan McQuillan to this place to save the souls of those poor children who die before the priest has administered the sacrament of baptism. From now on, those unfortunate souls do not have to wander in the black eternity of the In-Between Place. No! From now on, they may be lifted straight into Heaven. Those children will not have to be dug into the hedgerows or planted at crossroads, nor will they lie amongst the mouldering, murderous scum and drowned, drunken sailors in the killeen. Those children shall be buried in ground holier than that of any churchyard – indeed, those children shall be buried in the holiest ground on earth and their souls shall be saved!'

And then the people would clap their hands together and cry, 'Our God is merciful! We must spread this good news!'

And then Fillan McQuillan would put a bony finger to his thin lips, lower his voice and say, 'You may spread this news, but the priest must not know.' And then he would doff his hat and leave.

In a very short time, most everyone – except the priest – knew about the work of Fillan McQuillan. And, for seven years, Fillan McQuillan was kept mighty busy with the saving of unbaptised children's souls and the burying of their bodies.

>-+●>-0-<●+-<

When a woman birthed a dead child, she would send her husband to fetch Fillan McQuillan. After the sun had set, Fillan McQuillan would arrive at the grieving household with a horse and cart. He would slide all respectful into the house, look at the dead child and say, 'There is no sight that makes me sadder. I would be happy to take this child's body to the holiest ground on earth and save its soul this very night. Of course, a small contribution would greatly help the easing of this poor soul into Heaven.'

And then he would remove his hat and bow his bony body right down. He would place his hat in front of his feet, and the husband would fill the hat with coins. Fillan McQuillan would not pull himself upright until the hat was completely full. If Fillan McQuillan did not pull himself upright when the husband had finished putting coins into the hat, the husband would say, 'But these are all the coins we have!'

Then Fillan McQuillan would pull himself upright and hold up his hands and say, 'Oh, I do understand, but I'm afraid I will not be able to take your child to the holiest ground on earth and save its soul. However, I would be happy to take the child to the killeen tonight and lay it down with the mouldering, murderous scum and drowned, drunken sailors – it's the least I can do.'

And then the woman would cry, 'Oh, God have mercy on my child's soul!'

And then Fillan McQuillan would move his eyes all about the room until he found something he liked the look of and say, 'I have always admired those candlesticks,' or 'A table like that would sit well in my parlour,' or 'That picture deserves a finer setting.' In bigger houses, he would say, 'I've always liked your horses,' or 'I could do something with that big field of yours,' or 'No finer mirror have I ever seen'. And only when the husband gave him all the things he liked would Fillan McQuillan agree to take the child.

Then the husband would sometimes ask, 'Will we see you in chapel on Sunday?'

'Of course not!' Fillan McQuillan would answer, as if he

had been asked the most ridiculous question in the world. And then he would holy his bony hands together and look up to the sky and soften his voice and say, 'God has told me that, on Sundays, I must tend the graves of all the children who have been buried in the holiest ground on earth.'

And then Fillan McQuillan would take the child, wrap it in silk and leave, his hat full of coins and his cart often so full that his horse could barely pull it.

⊱────⊰

When a woman asked if she could visit the grave of her child, Fillan McQuillan would draw in a mighty fast breath and cup his bony hands around his bony face. Then he would shake his head furious fast and say, 'My dear woman, God has shown me the holiest ground on earth, a place that is so close to Heaven that you can hear the saints talking.

'God told me to keep this place a secret. He said that if everyone knew where the holiest ground was, then all sorts of riff-raff would try to squeeze their way into Heaven, and then He would have to *un*holy it. And if He unholied the ground, then anyone who had been buried there would have their souls sucked right out of Heaven and straight down into Hell. So, if you go to your child's grave, then you will surely send its soul to the Devil himself!'

And then the woman would sink to the floor and cross herself and weep, 'Oh, do forgive me, Fillan McQuillan. What a stupid thing for me to ask.'

And then Fillan McQuillan would sweeten his voice into a honey of sorts and put his bony hands to his heart and say, 'Have no fear, sweet woman. When I bury the body of your child, it will be wrapped in the finest silk, and the ground will be pleasingly herbed, and there will be an ivory grave cross carved by Saint Peter's own hands.

'The hand of God Himself will appear. His hand will take the soul of your child, and the angels will sing a lullaby to it, and a thousand flowers will spring up around the grave – even in winter. And then the soul of your child will play with the souls of the other children that have been saved, and God Himself will gentle the soul of your child and cosy it, and it will be at peace.'

And then the woman would turn to her husband and say, 'Isn't it wonderful, husband? May Fillan McQuillan be sainted a thousand times over, for there is no godlier man on earth!'

▻◅▸◦◂◦▸◅◃

But I am sorry to tell you that Fillan McQuillan was no godly man, and that God had not called him to do this work. In fact, Fillan McQuillan was not doing this work at all.

When Fillan McQuillan left the grieving households, he would drive his horse hard to the big white house on the Lannimore Hill. He would pour the coins into a large oaken chest, unhitch and unload his cart and unwrap the dead child. He would toss the dead child into a dirty sack, saddle up his fastest horse and then shove the sack into one of the saddlebags.

Then he would gallop inland to a place called McKinney's Murch, an overgrown, stagnant ditch that most everyone had forgotten about. He would empty the sack into the murch and then gallop home, making sure that he was back in the big white house before dawn.

For seven years, Fillan McQuillan's secret remained safe. The good people who lived on the coast between Colliery Bay and Portballintrae, and those who lived a fair way inland too, were all blissful happy because they thought that the bodies of their unblessed children had been buried in the holiest ground on earth and that the souls of their children had gone straight to Heaven.

If the good people had known that the bodies of their children were rotting in a heap in a stinking murch, and that the poor souls of their children were trapped in the black eternity of the In-Between Place, then they would not have been blissful happy at all.

Temptation

It was the clever habit of Fillan McQuillan to spend no longer than seven years in any one place. In thirty-five years, his crookedness had not been uncovered.

But Fillan McQuillan was growing old and tired, and he really liked the big white house on the Lannimore Hill. So, after seven years had passed, he decided that he would not move on as he had so many times before. Instead, he decided that he would tell people that the holiest ground on earth was too full to take any more bodies, and he would retire.

On the very day that Fillan McQuillan intended to tell people that he could no longer take their dead children, a man called Kearney O'Connell knocked on the door of the big white house and cried, 'A great fever is sweeping up the coast from Ballycastle! It has already burned through Carnduff, and my newborn son lies dead in my wife's arms. Please come to take him tonight!'

Fillan McQuillan did not have to think for very long to see how wealthy that fever could make him. He decided that he could retire after the fever had done its work – and that this unexpected epidemic would ensure that his later years would be very comfortable indeed.

So, instead of explaining to Kearney O'Connell that he

could not help, Fillan McQuillan holied his hands together and said, 'It is God's own wish that the soul of your poor child be saved. I will visit you after the sun goes down.'

><del>+·+••·+·-0-·+••·+·-<

After the sun had gone down, Fillan McQuillan arrived at Kearney O'Connell's cottage with a horse and cart. He slid all respectful into the cottage and looked at the dead child and said, 'There is no sight that makes me sadder. I would be happy to take this child's body to the holiest ground on earth and save its soul this very night. Of course, a small contribution would greatly help the easing of this poor soul into Heaven.'

And then Fillan MacQuillan removed his hat and bowed his bony body right down. He placed his hat in front of his feet, and Kearney O'Connell filled it up.

When Fillan McQuillan was satisfied with the coinage, he pulled himself upright and said, 'The soul of your child will be held in the arms of God Himself tonight.'

Kearney O'Connell's wife said, 'This brings me great comfort, Fillan McQuillan, but it would bring me even greater comfort to know that the body of my child will not lie all lonely in the ground. When you bury my son tonight, would you put a toy into his sweet and holy grave? My husband carved it himself.'

Now, it was not uncommon for people to ask for something to be buried with their child, and sometimes that something was of great worth. If it *was* such a something, then Fillan McQuillan took it for himself and sold it. If it was *not* such a something, then he threw it into the murch with the child.

Kearney O'Connell went to a small cabinet and fetched out a wooden figure that was the shape of a horse and the size of a working man's hand. It was roughly worked, sloppily painted and its ears were far too big for its head. One of its legs was much shorter than the others and its tail was a wee, tiny stump of a thing.

Fillan McQuillan took the toy and said, 'Be assured that this toy will be buried with your son.' And Fillan McQuillan was telling the truth.

Fillan McQuillan took the dead child and the toy, wrapped them in silk and left.

After leaving Kearney O'Connell's cottage, Fillan McQuillan drove his horse hard to the big white house on the Lannimore Hill. He put the coins into a large oaken chest and unhitched his cart from his horse. He unwrapped the dead child and the toy and then tossed them into a dirty sack. He saddled up his fastest horse and shoved the sack into one of the saddlebags. With the clear night sky lit bright by the harvest moon, Fillan McQuillan galloped off to McKinney's Murch.

When he got to the murch, he emptied the sack. Then he

got back on to his horse and galloped back to the big white house on the Lannimore Hill.

⪢─◆─○─◇─⪡

For the next three months, the fever burned up and down the coast, and a fair way inland too, and Fillan McQuillan profited well from it. When the fever had cooled, Fillan McQuillan declared his retirement. He explained that the holiest ground on earth was so full that it could not take another body, and while people did not want it to be true, they believed him.

And when people said, 'Well, at least you'll be able to come to chapel on Sundays now', Fillan McQuillan would say 'Of course not!' as if the people had said the most ridiculous thing in the world. And then he would holy his bony hands together and look up to the sky and soften his voice and say, 'It is God's own wish that, on Sundays, I continue to tend the graves of the children that have been buried in the holiest ground on earth. The Lord Himself will send down his most blessed saints to help me tidy the ground, and the angels with the sweetest voices will sing to the bones of the children while the work is done.'

And then he would pause and perfume his voice with righteous wholesome and say, 'And I will say the names of the children buried in the holiest ground on earth out loud, so that God remembers to comfort their souls best of all.'

And then the people would say, 'May Fillan McQuillan be sainted a thousand times over, for there is no godlier man on earth!'

⊱──⊰

And so, for the very first time, Fillan McQuillan did not move on.

But he should have moved on.

He should have moved out of the big white house on the Lannimore Hill.

He should have gone to a place where nobody knew him and where the people who lived on the coast between Colliery Bay and Portballintrae, and those who lived a fair way inland too, would never find him.

He should have moved on because, on the night he emptied the body of the O'Connell child into McKinney's Murch, he was being watched by the washerwoman of the Ballynagor Bridge.

Rescue

The washerwoman of the Ballynagor Bridge was a woman

who had died in childbirth but who was not all-the-way dead.

Because the priest had not been able to give the woman the birthing blessing before her death, her body had been buried in the killeen. Three faeries happened to be passing the killeen when the woman was being buried. They liked the look of her body, so they returned to the grave the next day, lifted it out of the ground and breathed a little life into it. They made the woman into a washerwoman and took her more than a fair way inland to the Ballynagor Bridge. They told her that the life that had been breathed into her would run out on the day she would have died had she survived the birthing of her child, and on the day the breath ran out, they would take her body back to the killeen.

By day, the washerwoman washed clothes in the Stracam River, under the Ballynagor Bridge. By night, she roamed the watery places of the countryside, looking for the child that had once grown in her belly.

Most everyone who saw the washerwoman was feary'd to their bones by the look of her. Her grey skin was all water-wrinkled, her hands were rubbed red-raw and her toes were all webbit. Her baldy head was covered in weeping sores, and her nose was boneless and flip-flapped all about her face. She had a single, long, sharp, yellow tooth that stuck out from her bottom gum and showed itself even when her mouth was closed. She was clothed in green from the waist down and bare from the waist up, and her breasts were long and heavy and all drippit with milk.

But, in spite of the feary look of the washerwoman, most everyone who saw her at the bridge summoned the courage to creep up on her and look at the clothes she was washing. They prayed all big and mighty that they would not see their own clothes being washed, because the clothes that she washed underneath the bridge were the grave clothes of a person who was about to die.

◄─►◦◄─►◦◦◄─►◄

On the night that Fillan McQuillan took the body of Kearney O'Connell's child to the murch, the washerwoman of the Ballynagor Bridge had roamed much further than usual in search of her child. She had waded out of the Stracam River and into the Black Water. From the Black Water she had slid across waterlogged fields to the Gortanuey moss. And from the Gortanuey moss she had heard a sound so sickening sad that it would have hurt a mortal's ears to hear it. But it did not hurt her ears – it comforted them. It was the sound of a hundred children or more calling for their mothers.

The washerwoman followed the sad sound and it took her to Mckinney's Murch. And I'm telling you the truth when I say that the smell from the murch was so horrible that it turned the washerwoman inside out and back again.

But the smell did not deter her, and she climbed right into the murch.

The butter-soft bodies of the dead children fell apart under her webbit feet and the souls of the dead children rose up in a grey mist from the murch and will-o'-the-wisped all about her and cried, 'Take me and love me, Mother!'

'Is my son here?' called the washerwoman, her voice full of hope.

'I will be your son, Mother!' cried the souls of the dead children. 'Take me and love me!'

'I will take one of you as my son tonight,' said the washerwoman. 'And I will love you and gentle you until my breath runs out. And after my breath runs out, I will love you even more. I will reach into the murch and lift a body, and, if it is yours, you must fly into it and stay in there so that I may hold you and so that you may feel the comfort of it.'

But just as the washerwoman bent over to lift a body, the mist of souls turned winter cold and dropped into the murch. In unison they whispered, 'He's coming, Mother.'

'Who is coming?' asked the washerwoman.

But the souls did not answer.

Moments later, the washerwoman could hear the thud of hard-galloping hooves and she crouched right down to hide herself. Soon enough, Fillan McQuillan appeared at the edge of the murch holding a dirty sack. The washerwoman saw Kearney O'Connell's son fall from the sack into the murch and she saw the wooden horse land next to him.

When Fillan McQuillan had gone, she saw the soul of the child leave its body. It started to cry and said, 'Where is my mother?'

'I am here, my darling son,' gentled the washerwoman. 'Now, you be a good boy and fly back into your body so I can take you home.'

When the soul of Kearney O'Connell's son was back in its body, the washerwoman lifted the dead child and lullabied it and kissed it and cosied it. Then she put the toy in the pocket of her skirt and carried the child back to the Ballynagor Bridge.

►─►─○─◄─◄

When the washerwoman got to the bridge, she sat herself down on a large rock at the edge of the river and put a drippit breast to the dead child's mouth. And as soon as a drop of milk touched the child's lips, the child opened its mouth wide and began to drink.

As the child drank, its heart started to beat and its body warmed a little. When it had finished drinking, it was no longer dead. And although it was not all-the-way alive, it was alive all the same.

The washerwoman rocked the child and stroked its cheeks and said, 'I will call you Caoimhín, and I promise to love you until my breath runs out. And after my breath runs out, I will love you even more.'

And the washerwoman kept her word.

Hope

Every morning for the next seven years, the washerwoman fed Caoimhín from her breast. And, in spite of taking no other form of nourishment, he grew into a boy of sorts.

With his mossy green skin, his head crowned with a wreath of golden bladderwort and his body all wrapped in rough rushes, you would have thought he'd be a fright to look at, but he wasn't. His eyes were so full of innocent, and his smile was so comely with wholesome, that you would have taken him for some kind of angel.

Every day for the next seven years, the washerwoman washed clothes under the Ballynagor Bridge and Caoimhín sat all secret and safe in the rushes and watched her.

One day, Caoimhín asked the washerwoman, 'Whose clothes do you wash, Mother?'

'These are the clothes of old farmer Brogan,' she answered.

'And why are you washing the clothes of old farmer Brogan?' asked Caoimhín.

'Because old farmer Brogan will die tonight and he will need clean clothes for his grave,' she answered.

And then the washerwoman told Caoimhín the story of old farmer Brogan. She told him how old farmer Brogan had cared for the land and his animals. She told him how he had been kind to many a stranger and how he had loved his wife and children.

Then Caoimhín asked, 'And what will happen to old farmer Brogan when he dies?'

'He was a good man, so his soul will surely go to Heaven,' smiled the washerwoman.

The next day Caoimhín asked the washerwoman again, 'Whose clothes do you wash, Mother?'

'These are the clothes of old lady Melville,' she answered.

'And why are you washing the clothes of old lady Melville?' asked Caoimhín.

'Because old lady Melville will die this afternoon and she will need clean clothes for her grave,' she answered.

And then the washerwoman told Caoimhín the story of old lady Melville. She told him how old lady Melville had pecked at her husband and cold-cruelled her children and complained about most everything you could think of. She told him how she had cheated and lied and shared a bed with a highwayman so he would shoot and steal for her.

Then Caoimhín asked, 'And what will happen to old lady Melville when she dies?'

'She was not a good woman, so her soul will surely go to Hell,' frowned the washerwoman.

After that, Caoimhín asked the washerwoman every day about the owner of the clothes she was washing. Every day, she would tell Caoimhín the story of the person and afterwards he would ask, 'And what will happen to them, Mother?' And she would say, 'Their soul will surely go to Heaven,' or 'Their soul will surely go to Hell,' and Caoimhín would nod his head and say, 'It surely will, Mother.'

Every night for the next seven years, the washerwoman took the wooden toy that Kearney O'Connell had made from her pocket and gave it to Caoimhín. As Caoimhín galloped the toy through the air, the washerwoman told him stories about the adventures of a horse called Dóchas.

The washerwoman would begin by saying, 'This is the story of how Dóchas swam across the mighty Atlantic,' or 'This is the story of how Dóchas won a battle for a king,' or 'This is the story of how Dóchas turned into a prince.' And she would keep talking until Caoimhín dropped the toy and fell asleep. And when he was asleep, she would cradle him and comfort him until the dawn came.

One crisp autumn morning, when a full seven years had passed, the washerwoman fed Caoimhín, as usual. Caoimhín sat all secret and safe in the rushes, and the washerwoman waded into the waters of the Stracam and started to wash clothes, as usual.

As Caoimhín watched, he noticed that she was washing a green skirt, rinsing a wreath of bladderwort and combing through a pile of rough rushes.

Caoimhín asked the washerwoman, 'Whose clothes do you wash, Mother?'

'These are the clothes of the washerwoman of the Ballynagor Bridge and of the young boy Caoimhín,' she answered.

'And why are you washing the clothes of the washerwoman of the Ballynagor Bridge and of the young boy Caoimhín?' asked Caoimhín.

'Because the washerwoman will die at sunrise tomorrow, and the young boy Caoimhín will die just after her, and they will both need clean clothes for their graves. The washerwoman's body will be buried in the killeen. Caoimhín will lie with his horse, Dóchas, in an open grave in the rushes under the Ballynagor Bridge, and his clean clothes will help him to lie as comfortably as he can.'

And then the washerwoman told Caoimhín the story of how she had once been a woman whose name she had long forgotten and how she had died in childbirth and how she had been buried in the killeen because the priest had not been able to give her the birthing blessing before her death. She told Caoimhín how three faeries had come to the killeen and taken her body and breathed a little life into it and made her into a washerwoman and how the breath would not last for ever.

And then the washerwoman told Caoimhín how, for thirty years, she had roamed at night looking for the child she had birthed and never found him. She told Caoimhín how, seven years ago, she had roamed much further than before and heard a hundred children or more calling for their mothers and how she had followed the sad sound and found the murch. She told Caoimhín how the murch was full of dead children and how a man had come on a horse and thrown a dead child and its toy horse into the murch and how she had taken the child and put it to her breast and given it a little life and called it Caoimhín.

She told Caoimhín that the milk from her breast kept him alive, and that, without the milk, he would die.

'And the washerwoman was kind and gentle and loved the boy Caoimhín. And she was a good woman. And the young boy Caoimhín loved the washerwoman and he was no trouble at all. And he was a good boy. So their souls will surely go to Heaven together,' smiled Caoimhín.

The washerwoman filled her voice to the brim with gentle and said, 'Without the birthing blessing, the washerwoman's body will be returned to the killeen and her soul will wander all about that unholy ground. Her soul will be trapped in the black eternity of the In-Between Place and it will ache for the company of the young boy Caoimhín. And while the soul of the young boy Caoimhín is filled with nothing but goodness, it will wander all about the Ballynagor Bridge. His soul will be trapped all lonely in the black of eternity of the In-Between Place because he did not receive the baptismal blessing.'

Caoimhín gripped the hands of the washerwoman tight and his eyes were so full of sad that, if you had seen them, your heart would have ached itself right out of your body.

The washerwoman took Caoimhín on to her lap and rocked him and cosied him and held her own tears in as best she could. As she closed her eyes and gentled him with a song, the breeze whipped up all about them and three beautiful voices joined the washerwoman's song. The air grew heavy with the unseasonal scent of lavender, the river stopped flowing, the rushes stopped swaying and the birds hung still-winged in the sky.

When the washerwoman stopped singing, she opened her eyes and saw, standing on the motionless river, the three faeries who had lifted her body from the killeen. White-eyed, white-skinned, white-haired and all cloaked in ermine, each looked the same as the other. One of the faeries opened her mouth to speak and three voices sounded at the same time.

'It is faerie law that whoever sucks at the breast of a washerwoman will be granted a single wish before they die,' the voices said. 'What is your wish, Caoimhín?'

'Can I wish for anything I like?' asked Caoimhín.

'You cannot wish that you do not die or that the washerwoman does not die, but you can wish big and clever all the same.'

A broad smile stretched right across Caoimhín's face and he jumped off the washerwoman's lap. His mossy, webbit feet spun him round in circles and his eyes sparkled all lively, and I am telling you the truth when I say that his wish was probably the biggest and cleverest wish that ever got made.

'Faeries, it is my wish that you take me and the washerwoman to a priest,' said Caoimhín.

The three faeries bowed slow and deep, and one of them spoke again in three voices and said, 'Your wish will be granted.'

The three faeries whirled themselves up into a white mist and sucked Caoimhín and the washerwoman into it.

The mist disappeared, the wings of the birds flapped free, the rushes started to sway again and the river flowed onwards.

At the side of the river, a new set of clothes appeared, but there was no one to wash them. And if you had seen those clothes, you would have thought they were the filthiest clothes that a body ever wore to the grave.

Truth

The white mist whip-whirled all the way to Ballycastle and

stopped outside the doors of the chapel. The three faeries bowed slow and deep to Caoimhín, and he bowed back.

The faeries whirled themselves up again into a white mist. The mist disappeared, and Caoimhín took the hand of the washerwoman and walked into the chapel.

Well, it just so happened to be a big holy day, and the chapel was fair bursting with people from up and down the coast and from a fair way inland too.

When Caoimhín and the washerwoman entered the chapel, the priest's jaw froze wide open and the people in the pews sucked in their breath and crossed themselves as fast as their hands would let them. None of them had ever been as far as the Ballynagor Bridge, and they had not seen the like of the washerwoman before.

An old woman stood up at the back of the chapel and said, 'It is surely a bad omen to see a hand from Heaven holding a hand from Hell.'

An even older woman stood up at the front of the chapel and shook her head and said, 'He is not from Heaven and she is not from Hell. That is a witch whose power is so strong that she has enchanted a handsome faerie and lain with him and borne his child.'

And the people in the chapel took the words of the older woman as true and crossed themselves all over again.

Caoimhín took the washerwoman to the front of the chapel. The people in the pews sat silent as Caoimhín looked up at the priest and said, 'I have come to ask you to give the baptismal blessing to me and the birthing blessing to this good woman so that our souls may go to Heaven.'

Before the priest could answer, a man stood up at the side of the chapel and shouted, 'Be gone from this chapel! No blessing will be given to a witch and its faerie child today!'

And one by one, people stood up and joined in the chant, 'Be gone! Be gone! Be gone!'

But Caoimhín took the priest's hand and eye-to-eyed him, and the priest could see the wholesome goodness in Caoimhín's eyes and fair took him for an angel. The priest raised his hand to stop the chant and the chapel fell silent again.

Caoimhín turned to face the people in the pews and said, 'This woman is not from Hell and she is not a witch and I am not her child.' And then Caoimhín told them the story of how the washerwoman had died in childbirth and how she had not received the birthing blessing and how she had been buried in the killeen. He told them how three faeries had breathed a little life into her body so that she was not all-the-way dead and how she had washed the clothes of those who were about to die and how she had gentled him and loved him as if he were her own child and how she would be all-the-way dead by the morning.

When Caoimhín had finished the story, he said, 'She has been a good woman and her soul should surely go to Heaven.'

And before the people from the pews could say a word, the priest put his hand on the washerwoman's head and gave the birthing blessing and said, 'It surely will.'

When the priest took his hand from the washerwoman's head, a white mist rose up from the ground and covered her. When the mist cleared, a beautiful old woman stood in the place of the washerwoman. A tumble of silvery curls danced all about her neck and shoulders. Her skin was paper thin and milky white and embroidered with fine threads from all sorts of stories. Her grey eyes glistened all steely bright.

'That is my wife, Maeve Mullen!' cried an old, grey-haired man from the centre of the chapel, pushing his way out of the pew to get to the front. When he got to Maeve Mullen, he put his coat around her bare shoulders and kissed her and said, 'I am your husband, Michael Mullen.' Then he called to the younger man who had been sitting next to him, 'Come and see your mother, Malachy!'

And Malachy Mullen fair ran to the front of the chapel and embraced his mother, and Michael Mullen said, 'Your son is a fine man, Maeve, and he has a good wife and three strong children. Look at them!' And the old, grey-haired man signalled for the rest of his family to come to the front of the chapel and embrace Maeve Mullen, and they did.

Maeve Mullen's heart was fair drunk with joy. The feel of her own child and grandchildren made her eyes teary up, and an ancient ache in her stopped. But while she was happy to be cosied and loved by her family, she had not forgotten Caoimhín. She gathered him in close to her and turned to face the people in the pews and said , 'Whilst I am certain that this child is not a faerie, I cannot be certain that he is not from Heaven.'

And then Maeve Mullen told them the story of how, seven years before, she had wandered to the Gortanuey moss and heard the sickening sad sound of a hundred children or more calling for their mothers. She told them how she had followed the sound to McKinney's Murch and how she had discovered the butter-soft bodies and aching souls of a hundred dead children or more.

Maeve Mullen told them how she saw a man come to the murch on a horse and open a sack and drop the body of a dead child into the murch. She told them how she had seen the child's soul leave its body and how she had told it to fly back in. She told them how she took the child and fed it until there was a little life in it. She told them how she had called the child Caoimhín and how she fed it every day to keep it alive and how the child would be all-the-way dead in the morning.

When Maeve Mullen had finished the story, she said, 'He has been a good boy and his soul should surely go to Heaven.'

And before the people from the pews could say a word, the priest wet Caoimhín's head and gave the baptismal blessing and said, 'It surely will.'

When the priest took his hand away from Caoimhín's head, a white mist rose up from the ground and covered him. When the mist cleared, a beautiful child stood in the place of the mossy boy. A mop of strawberry blond hair framed a freckled face and his cheeks glowed all bright and lively.

Caoimhín's innocent eyes scoured the chapel in the hope that someone would claim him just as Maeve Mullen had been claimed, but nobody did.

Instead, the people in the pews started horroring at the story of the murch. No one knew where the murch was, but most everyone took it to be a killeen of sorts, and they all started cursing and condemning the people who would not even give a dead child a blanket of earth for comfort.

Then the people in the pews kneeled right down and holied their hands together and started to pray.

Most of the people teary-smiled as they prayed: these were the people who were sending up big, silent, thank-you prayers for the work of Fillan McQuillan in days gone by. These were the people who were mighty glad that the bodies of their unbaptised children were lying all safe and warm in the holiest ground on earth and that the hand of God Himself had lifted the souls of their children into Heaven.

Some of the people grimmed and groaned as they prayed: these were the people whose unbaptised children had died after Fillan McQuillan had retired. They were sending up big save-a-soul prayers for their children whose small bodies were lying in the killeen or dug into a hedge or planted at a crossroads, and whose souls were trapped in the black eternity of the In-Between Place, just like the souls in the murch.

And every single one of those people prayed big and mighty that God Himself would soon make a new holy place for unbaptised children and that there would be plenty of space in that holy place and that He would call Fillan McQuillan to do His work for Him once again.

Though the people in the pews were terrible busy with the praying, Maeve Mullen cleared her throat to get their attention and said, 'Tomorrow morning, Caoimhín and I will be all-the-way dead. Now that we have both been blessed, our souls may travel to Heaven together and stay together. I wish to be buried in the chapel graveyard and for Caoimhín to lie next to me in the ground.'

Caoimhín nodded his head and said, 'Yes, I want to lie with Maeve Mullen, and I want to have Dóchas with me in the grave too.'

'Who is Dóchas?' asked the priest.

'On the night that Caoimhín was emptied out of the sack and into the murch, a small wooden horse fell out of the sack with Caoimhín's poor, little body. We call the horse Dóchas.' Maeve Mullen reached into the pocket of her skirt and pulled out the wooden horse.

'Let me see that horse!' demanded Kearney O'Connell, who was sitting in the front pew next to his wife.

Maeve Mullen gave the wooden horse to Kearney O'Connell, and he saw how it was roughly worked and sloppily painted and how its ears were far too big for its head. He saw how one of its legs was much shorter than the others and how its tail was a wee, tiny stump of a thing. There was no doubt in his mind that it was the very same horse he had given to Fillan McQuillan to be buried with his son.

Kearney O'Connell braved himself and said, 'And did the man on the horse wear a long black coat and a broad-brimmed hat in the Roman style?'

'He did,' answered Maeve Mullen.

A chill as deep and as sharp as midwinter ploughed through the pews of the chapel.

The eyes of Kearney O'Connell teary'd up, and he said, 'Seven years ago, I was promised that this wooden horse would be buried with my son in the holiest ground on earth. And, even though the fever burned the life out of my child before he could receive the baptismal blessing, I was promised that the hand of God Himself would lift my son's soul into Heaven.'

'Who made you these promises, Kearney O'Connell?' asked the priest.

Then, most every person in the chapel stood up and shouted, 'Fillan McQuillan!'

Justice

When the people in the chapel told the priest about the promises that Fillan McQuillan had made, the priest told the people in the chapel that no man could make such promises and that they had all been duped. He told them that the holiest ground on earth was certainly not to be found anywhere in the whole of Ireland and that no unbaptised soul would be allowed into Heaven.

The people in the chapel crackled with fury and roared scorch-a-soul curses.

Kearney O'Connell stood up on his pew and shouted, 'Fillan McQuillan shall swing from the gallows tree for this!'

And then most everyone in the chapel stamped their feet on the floor and chanted, 'Hang him! Hang him! Hang him!'

As the chilling chant grew louder, and the walls of the chapel fair shivered with the feary of it, Kearney O'Connell wrapped his arms around Caoimhín and claimed him as his son. And Caoimhín was mighty glad to be claimed even though he would be all-the-way dead by the morning.

Kearney O'Connell kissed his wife and told her to stay in the chapel with Caoimhín. Michael Mullen kissed Maeve Mullen and told her to stay in the chapel with Malachy Mullen and his wife and children.

And then Kearney O'Connell led the raging mob out of the chapel and off towards the big white house on the Lannimore Hill.

One hundred people or more tramped the seven-mile coastal road from Ballycastle to the Lannimore Hill. Those who had horses, including Kearney O'Connell and Michael Mullen, kept at the pace of the mob. Those who had carts let the weary folk rest in them when they needed to. Those who passed their own farms on the way to the Lannimore Hill collected pitch-forks and shovels. Some of the men carried pistols, and Kearney O'Connell collected a fat curl of rope from his cottage when the mob passed through Carnduff.

▻━◆━○━◆━◄

When the mob arrived at the bottom of the Lannimore Hill, Fillan McQuillan was not in his house but in the stable, tending his fine horses. Only when the mob was halfway up the hill did Fillan McQuillan hear it, and he did not like the sound of it at all. To the rhythm of its march, the mob was chanting:

> *We know about the murch, you broke your word:*
> *May your feet twitch and dance, old gallows bird!*

Careful not to show himself, he peered out of the stable, and when he saw the mob, he did not like the look of it either.

As quickly as he could, he saddled up his fastest horse, hopped up on it and hurtled out of the stables.

'There he goes!' cried a young woman from the mob.

The men with pistols shot at Fillan McQuillan, but his horse outran the bullets.

Fillan McQuillan did not head for the coastal road. Instead, he headed inland, riding hard over the rough flanks of the Lannimore Hill.

Kearney O'Connell and Michael Mullen galloped after him. The other men on horseback headed for the roads that hugged the edges of the hill in the hope of crossing his path. But Fillan McQuillan knew enough short cuts not to have to ride the roads at all. Soon the men on the roads gave up and returned to the big white house on the Lannimore Hill.

But Kearney O'Connell and Michael Mullen managed to keep Fillan McQuillan in their sights. They followed him over hedges, across fields, through woods and under bridges.

The sun slid down beneath the horizon, its glowing embers lingering until they were extinguished by a glittering night sky. The harvest moon shone brightly.

><+>-0-<+>-<

When Kearney O'Connell and Michael Mullen reached the edge of the Gortanuey moss, they saw Fillan McQuillan's horse whinny right up and throw him from the saddle. Fillan

McQuillan tried to get back on the horse, but the horse whirled round in circles and would not let him up.

As the horse whirled, the sky began to bend and bulge, and the air filled with the sickening sad sound of a hundred children or more calling for their mothers.

Kearney O'Connell and Michael Mullen left their horses at the edge of the moss. Kearney O'Connell slung the fat curl of rope over one of his shoulders and then the two men ran towards Fillan McQuillan.

When Fillan McQuillan tried to run, a grey mist rose up from the moss and wrapped itself all tight around him.

The mist lifted Fillan McQuillan into the air and then the sickening sad sound turned into a searing scream that was fit to burn a big hole in the night sky.

The mist started to move out of the moss.

Kearney O'Connell and Michael Mullen followed the mist to the edge of McKinney's Murch. And I'm telling you the truth when I say that, even though the bodies of the children were rotted down to their bare bones, the smell from the murch was so horrible that it turned Kearney O'Connell and Michael Mullen inside out and back again.

The mist will-o'-the-wisped all about Fillan McQuillan's body and a hundred children's voices or more chanted:

> *He carried us here and he threw us in,*
> *and he shall be cursed for this awful sin.*

We will cut him open and set his innards free,
and hang him up high from an alder tree.
We will chase out his breath and push out his eyes,
and rip out his soul in spite of his cries.
And his ears will be filled with howling from Hell:
old Fillan McQuillan will not rest well.

When the children's voices stopped chanting, Fillan McQuillan's eyes were blazit with fear, and he cried out to Kearney O'Connell and Michael Mullen for help. 'Oh, save me! I will repent! I will make amends!'

'Oh, there is no sight that makes us sadder than a man feary'd of the dying. We would be happy to save you from the mist this very night. Of course, a small contribution would greatly help the easing of you from your predicament,' said Kearney O'Connell, pulling a cap out of his pocket.

Kearney O'Connell bowed right down and placed the cap in front of his feet.

Fillan McQuillan said, 'I will give you the big white house on the Lannimore Hill. I will give you everything in the house. I will give you my stables and my horses and all my money.'

Kearney O'Connell did not pull himself upright.

'But that is all I have!' cried Fillan McQuillan.

Kearney O'Connell pulled himself upright and held up his hands and said, 'Oh, we do understand, but we're afraid we will not be able to save you tonight.'

And then the mist narrowed itself into a rough-edged blade and cut into Fillan McQuillan's body and carved out his innards all unskilful-slow.

And then the mist shaped itself into a snake and slithered over to Kearney O'Connell. The mist slipped the fat curl of rope from Kearney O'Connell's shoulder and slung it around Fillan McQuillan's neck and set him hanging from an alder tree.

And then the mist screamed its way into Fillan McQuillan's mouth and roared around inside his body and chased the breath right out of him. The mist pushed the eyes out of his head and then whip-whirled out of his mouth.

And then the mist shaped itself into a hand and reached into Fillan McQuillan's butchered body and snatched out his soul.

The soul was all black and shrivelled and the mist took it and stretched it until it screamed. And then the mist pulled it and prodded it and poked it until it pleaded for mercy. But the mist showed Fillan McQuillan's soul no mercy.

And then two funnels of fire roared their way up out of the murch and burned their way into Fillan McQuillan's ears, and his body floundered and flailed.

And then two more funnels of fire roared their way out of the murch and burned their way into Fillan McQuillan's soul, and his soul crisped and curled.

And then the mist dropped into the murch.

And then Fillan McQuillan's body stopped floundering and flailing because Fillan McQuillan was all-the-way dead.

And if you had seen his clothes, you would have thought that they were the filthiest clothes that a man ever wore to his grave.

⊱───────⊰

Kearney O'Connell and Michael Mullen rode as fast as they could to the Lannimore Hill. As they rounded the curve of Craignagolman, they saw that the big white house was roarit with flames.

When they got to the house, the crowd was standing in silence, watching the last traces of Fillan McQuillan disappear.

Kearney O'Connell said, 'Justice has been done.'

Heaven

Just as the light of a crimson dawn crept above the horizon, Kearney O'Connell and Michael Mullen arrived at the chapel in Ballycastle.

Kearney O'Connell's wife and Malachy Mullen and his

family were standing next to the priest at the edge of an open grave and their faces were fair soaked with the sad of it all.

Kearney O'Connell and Michael Mullen ran to the grave and saw Caoimhín and Maeve Mullen inside it. Caoimhín was sitting on Maeve Mullen's lap. He was holding Dóchas and making him gallop about in the air, and she was telling him the story of how Dóchas went to Heaven.

Kearney O'Connell leaned into the grave and kissed his son.

Michael Mullen leaned into the grave and kissed his wife.

And when Maeve Mullen finished the story, she lay down and closed her eyes and died. And then Caoimhín lay his head on Maeve Mullen's chest and closed his eyes and let go of Dóchas and died too.

><+>-○-<+><

Now most people say that this is where the story ends. But there are some people who remember the old times, and they will tell you that this is not where the story ends at all.

The people who remember the old times will tell you that, at the very moment the boy Caoimhín let go of Dóchas, a shroud of the finest white silk drifted down from the sky and wrapped itself around the bodies of Maeve Mullen and Caoimhín O'Connell. They will tell you that the earth inside the grave was greened with the most pleasing herbs and that

Saint Peter appeared and planted an ivory grave cross that had been carved by his own hand. And they will tell you that the hand of God Himself appeared and that His hand took the souls of Caoimhín O'Connell and Maeve Mullen up into Heaven, and that the air was filled with the sound of angels singing lullabies, and that a thousand flowers sprang up around the grave.

The people who remember the old times will also tell you that if you see three white-eyed, white-skinned, white-haired women all cloaked in ermine standing at the chapel gate, you must not look them in the eye. They will tell you that those three women are faeries waiting to take Maeve Mullen's body to the killeen, and that if you let them cast an enchantment in your eye, they'll take your body instead.

And they will also tell you that if you go to McKinney's Murch just after the sun goes down, you will see the ghost of Fillan McQuillan swinging from an alder tree.

Now, I heard this story from Bridie Brogan who remembers the old times and was once an O'Connell herself. And she told me that this is a true story, and that anyone who hears it would do well to believe it.

SEACHMALL

On Saint Agatha's feast, when the moon was bursting full and the snowdrops were fast asleep, a fisherman's daughter called Síomha slipped out of her bed and off to the rocks that lie close to the harbour at Dunseverick.

When she got to the rocks, she took off her shoes and picked her way to her favourite place – a large, flat, glistening platform of basalt that jutted right out into the sea. She sat down on the edge, gathered her long, winter cloak tight around her and looked up at the brightly polished night sky and down at the soft, bulging curves of the deep, dark sea. She pulled her knees close to her chest and let her body rock to the comforting, rhythmic thud of the waves against the harbour wall. And then she spoke into the cold, still air.

'Oh, what am I to do?' she asked, her words turning to mist as they left her mouth and her eyes puddling with tears.

'About what, my dear?' replied a voice that fair twinkled with the lively.

Síomha jumped to her feet in surprise and looked around for the owner of the voice.

'I'm down here!' cried the voice.

An enormous salmon leapt out of the water and slapped itself down on to the rock next to Síomha's feet. His silver-blue back sparkled in the moonlight and, if you had seen him with your own eyes, you would have taken him for the most handsome fish in the sea.

'I am Seachmall, and I'm on my way to meet my wife in the River Bann. I was just taking a wee rest in this lovely spot,' said the salmon.

Again, the salmon leapt up in the air, this time whirling around and showing Síomha the full plump of his shiny, white belly. He landed on his powerful tail fins and bowed right down, then he stretched himself up as far as he could and said, 'I have been at sea for a full five years and in that time I have experienced many things.

'I have wrestled with the mighty kraken in the black waters by Greenland. I have been loved by the blue-tailed merrowmaids of the great Gulf of Bothnia. I have learned from a thousand wise men who knew how to speak the truth. I have watched battles won and lost. I have heard the endless ache of a grief that will not die and I have seen how bitterness can burn a man alive. In short, my dear, I'd wager that I'm long enough salted to offer you some words of advice. Now tell me, what is it that ails you so?'

Síomha sat down again and pushed back the hood of her cloak, letting waves of long red hair fall about her shoulders. And then she told Seachmall all about her sorry predicament.

She told him how a fine-looking nobleman had approached her at the Lammas Fair and how that nobleman had sweetened his voice with talk of her great beauty and asked her to lie with him.

'And did you lie with him?' asked Seachmall.

'No, I did not,' answered Síomha.

And then Síomha told Seachmall how the fine-looking nobleman had come to the gate of her father's cottage at the harvest moon and how that nobleman had sweetened his voice with talk of love and asked her again to lie with him.

'And did you lie with him?' asked Seachmall.

'No, I did not,' answered Síomha.

And then Síomha told Seachmall how the fine-looking nobleman had climbed into her bed at Hallowmas and how that nobleman had sweetened his voice with a promise of marriage and asked her again to lie with him.

'And did you lie with him?' asked Seachmall.

'Yes, I did,' answered Síomha.

'And did he marry you?' asked Seachmall.

'No, he did not,' answered Síomha. 'I took him for an honest man, but he was not as he seemed. The day after I lay with him, he married a wealthy woman from Ballintoy. And one moon after I lay with him, I learned that I was carrying his child. And now three moons have passed and the child still grows inside me. My clothes squeeze me tighter by the day and my father will soon see the truth of things. What am I to do?'

'My dear,' gentled Seachmall, 'I know exactly what you should do, and I would be happy to answer your question – as long as you can answer mine first.'

'What is your question?' asked Síomha, a splash of hope in her voice

Seachmall narrowed his glassy, black eyes and flip-flapped his belly fins and darkened his voice and said, 'You say that you took the nobleman for an honest man, but he was not as he seemed.'

Síomha nodded.

Then Seachmall spun a full turn on his tail fins and widened his glassy, black eyes and smalled his voice down to a whisper and said, 'My dear, my question is – what if nothing is at it seems?'

As Seachmall waited for Síomha's answer, he tick-tocked his head from side-to-side and drummed his tail fins on the rocks. But, try as she might, Síomha could not bend her mind to the shape of his question, and after a while, she said, 'Your question is vexing me and I fear I cannot answer it. Might you be kind enough to answer my question without me answering yours?'

Seachmall's gills flared ferocious-fast and he shook his head all sad and slow. 'No, my dear. I am sorry to say that I cannot answer your question until you have answered mine.'

'Oh, what am I to do?' cried Síomha again into the cold, still air. And when no answer came, she sobbed and she sobbed until her face was all soaked and her eyes were all misted with tears. And if you had seen her face with your own eyes, you would have taken it for the saddest face that was ever made.

Indeed, Seachmall's own eyes watered right up at the sad and sorry of it, and he took pity on Síomha and said, 'Wipe the tears from your eyes, my dear. Then look at your tears and tell me what you see.'

Síomha did as he said and wiped the tears from her eyes. Then she examined her hand.

'I see only my wet palm,' said Síomha, bursting into another bout of sobbing.

'Look again,' said Seachmall, thunder-slapping his tail fins on the rocks.

This time, as Síomha looked at her palm, she saw her tears turn into a handful of sparkling sapphires.

'Did you cast an enchantment on my tears, Seachmall?' asked Síomha, scarcely able to contain her delight.

'No, my dear, I did not,' answered Seachmall. 'It is your own eyes that enchant the world and turn it into something it is not. I have merely broken the enchantment of your eyes so that you may see the world as it really is.'

And then Síomha looked up at the moon. And, as she looked at it, she saw it turn into a beautiful silvery woman. The silvery woman smiled at Síomha and sang to her. The stars joined in with the singing and swayed from side to side. And, if you had heard that sound with your own ears, you would have taken it for the heavenly harmony of God's own choir.

The sound reached into Síomha's heart and cradled it and comforted it and warmed the insides of her right up. And then the silvery woman shone as bright as the midsummer sun and warmed the outsides of Síomha right up too.

Síomha took off her winter clothes and lay down on the rocks and bathed in the warm of it all.

And then Síomha sat up and looked at her legs. And as she looked at them, she saw them turn into a single fishtail. She moved her tail to and fro and admired how the scales shimmered all green and sparkled all blue, and how shining pearls fell from her tail whenever she moved it. And, if you had seen that tail with your own eyes, you would have taken it for the powerful tail of the mighty Maarit, merrow queen of the Barents Sea.

And then Síomha leapt up in the air and whirled around and landed on her powerful tail fins. And as she looked out into the dark, bulging sea, she saw the water rise up into the shape of a strong, young man. She saw the man beckon her and the beautiful, silvery woman in the sky lit a path from the rocks straight into his arms.

She heard the man call her name and whisper noble promises to her, and if you had heard his words with your own ears, you would have taken them for the kindest, truest words that were ever spoken.

And then Seachmall winked at Síomha and said, 'Now, my dear, are you sure you cannot answer my question?"

And then Síomha spun a full turn on her tail fins and widened her watery, blue eyes and smalled her voice down to a whisper and said, 'Not only do I have the answer to your question, Seachmall – I have the answer to mine too.'

And then Síomha leapt into the sea.

><+>—O—<+>—<

When the sun reddened the morning sky and the snowdrops were wide-awake, a fisherman slipped out of his bed and off to the harbour at Dunseverick.

When he got to the harbour, he pulled his fishing boat out of its groundsel-edged nook and down to the top of the slipway. But he did not push the boat into the water because there on the slipway lay the naked body of a girl, her feet caught in a net.

The fisherman went to the girl and pushed her wet, red hair away from her face.

Her eyes stared all lifeless at him: sapphires without sparkle.

The round of her ripening belly traced the beginning and end of a new, small life: a promise unfulfilled.

Her skin was mottled all bluish-grey: unpolished pearls.

And in the net around her feet lay the clean, white bones of a long-dead salmon.

The fisherman sat down next to the body and gathered his skin coat tight around him. He looked up at the brightly painted morning sky and down at the soft, bulging curves of the deep, dark sea. He pulled the girl's body to his chest and rocked it to the comforting, rhythmic thud of the waves against the harbour wall. And then he spoke into the cold, still air.

'Oh, what am I to do?' he asked, his words turning to mist as they left his mouth and his eyes puddling with tears.

Some notes on the stories

The stories in this collection follow many conventions associated with traditional, oral storytelling. For this reason, as well as enjoying the stories in the privacy of your own head, you might also find that they're even better when read aloud and shared with others.

The Faerie Thorn

In Ireland, lone hawthorns are known as faerie thorns and are highly respected trees. People avoid uprooting them for fear of upsetting the faeries. It is believed that bad luck, illness, injury and death are all possible consequences of disrespecting the faeries and their trees.

Gowl is an Ulster-Scots word meaning howl, shout or bellow.

The Story of Amergin

This is a retelling of a story from the ancient Ulster Cycle, one of the four great cycles of Irish mythology. The stories in the Ulster Cycle focus on the exploits of the legendary heroes Cú Chulainn and Conchobar mac Nessa.

The pookah, or *púca*, is an Irish shape-shifting faerie that is thought to bring both good and bad fortune to farming and fishing communities. The look and behaviour of this faerie varies by region – appearing as an animal (often a black horse, goat or rabbit), as a human with animal features (such as a tail or snout), or as a wrinkled, deformed goblin.

In the original version of this story from the Book of Leinster, when Amergin speaks for the first time, he repeats a phrase three times: Does Greth eat curds? In English, these words don't seem too impressive, but in Irish they are very clever. The Irish word for curds is *gruth*: Amergin's first words are a pun on Greth's name.

The Salmon of Knowledge is a myth that features in the Fenian Cycle of Irish mythology. In this story, an ordinary salmon eats nine hazelnuts that fall into the Well of Wisdom and gains all the world's knowledge. The first person to eat the salmon's flesh will, in turn, acquire all of this knowledge.

The Merrow of Murlough Bay

Merrow is an Irish–English term for a mermaid or merman.

There are two Murlough Bays in Northern Ireland: one in County Down and one in County Antrim, where this story is set.

On a small hill close to the bay lie the ruins of an ancient church, said to have been built by Saint Moiloge (also known as Malock, Mologue and Mollock). Murlough is a corruption of the saint's name.

According to local legend, the clay from Malock's grave has healing qualities, but no one knows where the grave is.

The Song of Hulva

Breen Wood is a native oak wood near Ballycastle in County Antrim. It is one of the few remaining ancient woodlands in this part of the world and it is believed that it has survived this long because its name means faerie wood – and no one would dare cut down a wood that might belong to faeries.

In ancient Celtic tree lore, the holly and the oak are often depicted as two kings that battle every year, the holly always winning the battle for the dark part of the year, and the oak always winning the battle for the light part of the year.

Banagher Glen, near Dungiven, is home to ancient oak woodland too, and Tieveragh faerie hill is just outside Cushendall.

The Spirit of the Meadow Burn

The Bonner Mill (originally Curry's Mill) in Bushmills is said to be haunted by the ghost of a man who fell into the water wheel and drowned.

The four tasks set by Breewa are borrowed from an Old Norse myth in which Thor, Loki and Þjálfi are challenged by Útgarða-Loki.

In 1784, Hugh Anderson registered the Old Bushmills Distillery. Its trademark is a pot still.

Saint Columb's Rill is famed for supplying the distillery with water. The rill was originally called the Meadow Burn and did not get its new name until the late eighteenth century. Local legend has it that Saint Columba passed by the burn and blessed it. The blessing made the water sweet, and that's why the whiskey tastes so good.

Drookit is an Ulster-Scots word meaning drenched or extremely wet.

The Terrible Tale of Fillan McQuillan

A killeen, or *cillín*, is an unconsecrated burial ground that was used to inter unbaptised children, women who had not been 'churched' after childbirth, sailors and unrepentant murderers. Some killeens are more than a thousand years old.

Rural burial practices for unbaptised children maintained a sense of ritual. The killeens were usually relatively small and individual plots were sometimes marked with a simple stone. The body of the unbaptised child would be buried by its father between sunset on the day of its death and sunrise the following day. It wasn't until 1969 that the Catholic Church introduced funeral rites for unbaptised infants.

'Churching' is a ceremony in which a blessing is given to mothers after recovery from childbirth. Today, the blessing is usually a form of thanksgiving. In the past, in some traditions, the blessing was also considered to be a form of purification.

Murch is a local word for a march ditch (a boundary ditch).

The washerwoman is a type of *bean sídhe* or banshee.

Technically, the washerwoman, or *bean nighe*, is a Scottish faerie, but the Irish banshee is her natural counterpart. The spirit of a woman who died in childbirth, she is an omen of death and a messenger from the Otherworld. She washes the blood from the grave-clothes of those who are about to die and is cursed to wash until the day she would have died had she survived childbirth. According to tradition, if a mortal sucks the breast of a washerwoman, he can claim to be her foster child and make a wish.

Seachmall

Saint Agatha was a virgin martyr, and her feast day is 5 February. Agatha dedicated her life to God and desisted from marriage and sexual relationships. A Roman prefect called Quintianus made advances towards her, but she rejected him. He was so angry that he had her imprisoned and tortured, and she eventually died from her injuries. A vision of Saint Peter is said to have appeared to her shortly before her death, comforting her and filling her prison cell with heavenly light.

The Lammas Fair has taken place in Ballycastle every year at the end of August since the seventeenth century.

Glossary of names

Alva an anglicisation of the Irish name Ailbhe, meaning white

Amergin an anglicisation of the Irish name Aimhirghin, meaning born of song

Asna an anglicisation of the Irish name Easnadh, meaning musical sound

Bardán an Irish name, meaning poet or bard

Breewa a corruption of the Irish word *bríomhar*, meaning lively or vigorous

Caoimhín an Irish name, meaning heavenly birth; or noble child, gently born

Crann the Irish word for tree

Dara an anglicisation of the Irish name Dáire, meaning oak tree, dark oak, fruitful or fertile

Dervla an anglicisation of the Irish name Deirbhile, meaning daughter of a poet

Dóchas the Irish word for hope

Fillan an anglicisation of the Irish name Faolán, meaning little wolf

Gelace an anglicisation of the Irish name Geiléis, meaning bright swan

Hulva a corruption of the Old Norse word *hulfr*, meaning holly

Lusk a corruption of the Irish word *loisc*, meaning burn

Malock a version of an Irish saint's name which also appears as Moiloge or Mollock

Maarit a Finnish name, meaning pearl

Seachmall the Irish word for illusion

Síomha an Irish name, meaning good peace

Shan a corruption of the Irish word *sean*, meaning old

Smeench a corruption of the Irish word *smaointe*, meaning thought

Acknowledgements

A huge thank you to my friends and family for being a constant source of encouragement and support, and for reminding me to eat and sleep.

A special thank you to my editors, Patsy Horton and Kerri Ward at Blackstaff Press, for their enthusiasm and professionalism, and for teaching me the art of letting go.

And a respectful thank you to the faeries who live under the faerie thorn on our farm, without whom this book would not exist.